THE GREAT FIRE OF LONDON

Other Phoenix Fiction titles from Chicago

The Bridge on the Drina by Ivo Andrić
Concrete by Thomas Bernhard
Gargoyles by Thomas Bernhard
The Lime Works by Thomas Bernhard
Woodcutters by Thomas Bernhard
The Department by Gerald Warner Brace
Lord Dismiss Us by Michael Campbell
The Last, Long Journey by Roger Cleeve
Acts of Theft by Arthur A. Cohen
A Hero in His Time by Arthur A. Cohen
In the Days of Simon Stern by Arthur A. Cohen
Solomon's Folly by Leslie Croxford
The Old Man and the Bureaucrats by Mircea Eliade
Fish by Monroe Engel
In the Time of Greenbloom by Gabriel Fielding
The Birthday King by Gabriel Fielding
Through Streets Broad and Narrow by Gabriel Fielding
Concluding by Henry Green
Pictures from an Institution by Randall Jarrell
The Survival of the Fittest by Pamela Hansford Johnson
The Bachelor of Arts by R. K. Narayan
The English Teacher by R. K. Narayan
Swami and Friends by R. K. Narayan
Bright Day by J. B. Priestley
Angel Pavement by J. B. Priestley
The Good Companions by J. B. Priestley
Golk by Richard Stern
A Use of Riches by J. I. M. Stewart
The Painted Canoe by Anthony Winkler

THE GREAT FIRE
OF LONDON

PETER ACKROYD

THE UNIVERSITY OF CHICAGO PRESS

The University of Chicago Press, Chicago 60637

Originally published 1982
University of Chicago Press edition 1988
Printed in the United States of America

97 96 95 94 93 92 91 90 89 88   5 4 3 2 1

Library of Congress Cataloging in Publication Data

Ackroyd, Peter.
  The great fire of London.

  (Phoenix fiction)
  Reprint. Originally published: 1982.
  I. Title.   II. Series.
PR6051.C64G7   1988   823'.914   88-20838
ISBN 0-226-00264-0 (pbk.)

For Brian Kuhn

PART ONE

the story so far

Little Dorrit, born in the Marshalsea prison, has lived there with her father for many years. He had been imprisoned for a small debt, but has now lost the will to rescue himself from his confinement. Although her father is a prisoner, Little Dorrit herself, known as the 'Child of the Marshalsea', can enter and leave the prison as she wishes. She is forced to find work in order to support her father, and is given employment in the household of the Clennams, a mercantile family over whom there hovers a dark and terrible secret – of which, it seems, Little Dorrit is an unwitting part. Arthur Clennam, the son of the household, determines to assist Little Dorrit and her father in any way he can. With the help of Pancks, an agent, he discovers that the Dorrits are in fact heir to a great fortune. As a result, they are released from the Marshalsea with much celebration – although Little Dorrit faints as she is taken away from what, after all, is the only life she has ever known. She must leave behind, also, her only friend, 'Little Mother', a half-wit who has always relied upon her.

This is the first part of the novel which Charles Dickens wrote between 1855 and 1857. Although it could not be described as a true story, certain events have certain consequences....

one

Little Arthur is asleep, with the same expression he has had
for forty years. No one has ever seen it – it is the look of a man
who knows he is sleeping by himself. A fly is buzzing by the
window. The sun has just risen above the brick roofs, and the
fly rises from its torpor. And now it arouses Little Arthur with
its plaintive note. He sits on the edge of his bed, his feet not
touching the floor, immobile, like a photograph. Then he
jumps down and goes over to open the window. With infinite
care he shepherds the fly out into the morning air. It is,
however, a chilly London autumn and the fly will not last
long outside. The fly knows this, too, but still it wants to
escape.

Little Arthur stands upon a chair in order to wash himself
properly at the kitchen sink. He had stopped growing when
he was eight. He had lamented this fact for several months,
crying and talking to himself at the same time. And then,
suddenly, he no longer cried; a carapace had formed between
him and the world of ordinary feeling. He fills the kettle.
From his window he looks down upon a familiar scene: the
backs of other houses, other windows with their curtains
drawn, the small gardens with their stunted shrubs and
bushes. While he waits for the kettle to boil, he says good
morning and how are we today to the girl above his head. It is
in fact a photograph of a young girl, cut out from the local
newspaper. The face is so calm and clear, he will keep it for
ever. He has varnished it to the wall to prevent it from
turning yellow and indistinct.

Little Arthur is the proprietor of Fun City, a small
amusement arcade in Borough High Street, under an old and
now disused railway bridge. At 8.00 on the dot, he walks
down the High Street, with his peculiar rolling gait, looking
straight ahead, not glancing up. The newspaper seller,

wearing an old flat cap as if it were an extension of his cranium, knows him.

'How are we keeping this morning then, Arthur?'

'Oh, we keep, don't we, we keep.' He will not look up at him.

'Fun City' is displayed in a series of light bulbs but, to Little Arthur's knowledge, they have never been lit; unless, he thinks, they turn them on when he is asleep. Inside, in the early morning, the Fun Palace is like a dead star, without the bright notes of the pinball machines, the rattle of the coins, the simulated roar of the Auto Drive Cruiser, and the fake fire of the automatic rifles.

At 8.15 Little Arthur unlocks his office, at the back of the arcade, to switch on the electric current. He lets his right hand, his arm stretched fully in order to reach the red lever, hover for a moment. This is the moment of his triumph, when the powers of the earth enter Fun City and turn it into his magic cave. The hum begins and he hums along with it, and there is a light in Fun City more brilliant than the daylight. Little Arthur struts from machine to machine, reaches up to polish the glass cases, shine the metal knobs, inwardly preparing himself to meet the gaze of them. He sits on his wooden chair, his back against the wall, and watches the street.

It is then that he sees the letter, tossed casually into a corner. Letters mean trouble, they are the same as talk. He puts the kettle on, and then tears open the envelope.

It is from Leisure and Amusement Products Limited:

Dear Mr Feather,

We regret to inform you that, commencing 5 November, of this year, it has become regretfully necessary to terminate the lease of 'Fun City', 19 Borough High Street, London SE1. This is part of our rationalisation procedure, and in no way reflects your work on behalf of Leisure and Amusement Products Ltd. We will be in touch with you further regarding this concern, and concerning our obligations as they regard you.

He reads the letter over and over, concentrating each time

upon a different sentence. The breath leaves Little Arthur's body in great leaps. He can see his reflection, flattened and bent, in the glass front of the Auto Drive Cruiser. He tries hard to think of the little girl above his bed. But nothing calm comes. The kettle shrieks behind him. 'There's going to be conversations about this,' he says out loud. His hands move over his body, as if trying to press it into another shape. 'There's going to be electricity.' He hardly knows what he is saying.

two

Audrey Skelton lay in bed and looked at the ceiling. If she could have as many pounds as days like this, she would be rich. Quite rich, anyway, Rich enough. To get out of this dump. Audrey was a Russian princess, who had been forced to flee during the Revolution. She was a poetess who did not want her work to be discovered in her life-time. She was a mystery to those who knew, and loved, her best.

Audrey often dreamed like this during the day, in the sense that she play-acted. She would become someone other than herself – a millionairess, an actress, an opera singer – and she would imagine the life of that person in such attentive detail that she lapsed into a kind of trance. When she came home, after her shift at the telephone exchange, she would turn on the stereo and dance frantically to the music, so that the windows rattled. As she danced she would unpin her hair – red, luxuriant, which no hairdresser or perm had been able to tame – and it would trail around her like a circle of flame. She became, as it were, possessed.

But now she lay upon the bed, the day behind her as grey and cracked as the ceiling, when Tim knocked tentatively upon the front door. Since they were both in their early twenties, they maintained a certain distance, still sizing up each other for the main event – a possible life together. Audrey greeted Tim with a self-conscious languor, which he pretended not to notice. 'Hello there, Aud, just paying a quick visit, like.'

'Come on in then, Timothy Coleman, don't stand there gawping.' She looked exhausted, as though someone were spinning away her life.

'How's tricks then, Aud. Everything all right, is it?'

'I'm tired, Tim, that's all. Dog tired.'

He switched on the television, apologetically almost, as if

ne were injecting a note of false levity. There was some sort of drama concerning firemen; the red engines were speeding down the alleys and side-streets of London, sirens sounding, bells ringing. The same scenes had been the staple of television for many years; they were as predictable as a child's fantasy and yet, strangely, most people watched until the end.

Audrey ignored the television. 'Tim, did you know there used to be an old prison round here? Margery at work was telling me. You know, the one with the spots. It's just off the high street.' Tim knew vaguely. He was used to Audrey picking up something she had heard, or read, and elaborating upon it. He nodded without looking at her.

'You know where it was then, clever guts? Just down on the right by the supermarket. I must have passed there a thousand times and never knew. Strange, really.' Tim was watching to see if the fire could be halted before it destroyed some wharves by the river. He couldn't make up his mind whether they were using a set, or whether these were pictures of a real fire. It puzzled him.

'I wouldn't mind reading about it, Tim, I wouldn't really. History is interesting when you live in the area, isn't it?' She nudged him, and he squeezed her elbow without moving his head. 'Strange, really, to think of it on your doorstep like that. And now there's a supermarket.' Audrey sighed, and turned towards the screen.

They decided, for a bit of a change, to play the 'juke-machines', as Audrey insisted on calling them, in Fun City. And so into the dark streets they went, walking across shadows, scuttling against the wind which tried to push them back. Into the amusement arcade.

'Evening, Arthur. How's business, my old mate?'

Little Arthur, who was sitting on his wooden chair at the back of the arcade, seemed to smile back at Tim. He was always smiling. People worse off than you even, Audrey used to say, and they can still smile. It makes you stop and think. For her, Fun City was a kind of parable.

They played desultorily for a while. Audrey preferred the Love Bug; it was less complicated than the others and it let

9

off a pleasant low note, like a moan, whenever she won an extra ball. But tonight, when she touched the metal sides, she thought she received a slight shock, a jolt. But Little Arthur seemed to be watching her, and she said nothing. It might be her hair. Full of static. Tim was on Pirate Adventure, ducking and weaving, banging his hips against the machine, slapping its sides. I wish, Audrey thought, he would do that with me sometimes. Then, suddenly, Little Arthur was out of his chair and beside him, kicking Tim's shoes.

'Don't treat it like that, you! Where's the beauty of it when you bang it, you!' Tim and Audrey were astonished; Little Arthur had never been known to speak to a customer unless first addressed, and he had certainly never abused one before. 'Get away from it now, you! It's off. I'm turning it all off.'

Tim stared at Arthur as he had stared at the television: he did not know if this was real, or something made up, a game. It was something in between, something he did not have the words for.

Audrey took Tim's arm, and pulled him away from the machine. 'Come on, love,' she said, ignoring Little Arthur, 'It's getting parkey in here anyway. Let's get on home.'

They slept together that night, but they did not make love. Audrey 'felt funny'. She dreamed that she was inside the old prison, except that it was lit up by rows of brilliant lights. Little Arthur was showing her some photographs. She kept on asking him where her father was; he had spent all their money. She had to find him before something terrible happened.

three

When had the idea first occurred to Spenser Spender? That was the question people asked afterwards. It had come in a sentence – 'I never should have touched you, but I thought you were a child'. He could not remember the book but he knew that he would, when he needed to. It was a Sunday afternoon, and the faint sounds of the television wrapped themselves around Spenser Spender. He had come back here because of the prison. He was a film-maker. He had made a film about an inmate, and how his freedom had destroyed him. He had come back to look at the prison again, linger in front of it, calmly, so that it became real.

No, this was not really why he was here. He had come back because it was in this area that he had been born, that he had 'grown up'. He wanted to find a key to the mystery, although he did not yet know what the mystery was.

If you live beside a prison, he thought, you never notice it. But everything around it seems dead – the streets, the tiny front gardens, the red brick houses like mediaeval ovens, all dead or decaying. Even when he was a child, it had been like this; only then it had been more threatening, since it had seemed to be the condition of the world. Dead. All of it – as though the neighbourhood had held its breath for too long.

And they were still in there, they always had been, the inmates, lying on their small beds, inside. In his film they had been curiously self-revealing, as if they were drugged, or hypnotised, by their fates. These men had lost everything, but their fall had broken them open. 'I never should have touched you, but I thought you were a child.' Where was it? What was it from?

As Spenser Spender walked along the road outside the prison, he recognised someone who was hastening towards him. His name was Pally, something like that. They had lived

11

in adjoining streets and had gone to the same damp, melancholy school. But Pally would probably not have recognised Spenser even if he had seen him; he was simple – or so everyone said – and the apparent haste came from a nervous disjointedness in all of his movements. His face was too large for his head, and it seemed as though his eyes had gone out – as the wind might blow out two candles. There was spit on his chin, Spenser noticed, as Pally rushed by. He had known him for fifteen or sixteen years – the first years of their lives – and now they passed each other as though a third person was walking between them.

And then he remembered, and the idea came. It was so simple, he said later – it was from the book he had read at school, the book with the prison, the book with the girl. It was *Little Dorrit*. He remembered it now only as a series of engravings in a large. cloth-bound edition, and he remembered the sensations of intense fear which they had provoked in him – the houses packed together like sepulchres, the young girl like a pin-point of light hastening along a river bank, the prison yard, and then one face – a mad, blank face. He had been waiting for that face all his life.

This would be the film. He would make a film of *Little Dorrit*, using the real prison as his model. Wasn't it too vast a subject, they were to ask him? But he knew he had it in his power to raise up images; he could make people curse, or bless, whatever he cared to show to them; he could create darkness upon a screen, and then fill it with light.

Now he had a theme – and it was London itself, wasn't that it? – which could draw him further forward, eliciting pictures aı.ɟ images, probing the mystery. He wanted to call after Pally, and tell him that he understood now what had previously baffled him – the mystery was in the two of them, how they had passed each other. But Pally had turned a corner, hurrying away with his own indistinct thoughts.

Now Spenser ran to keep up with this new sensation of himself. He slipped and fell, without really noticing that he had done so. He wanted to tell someone about *Little Dorrit*. But he knew that the only person he could tell was his wife – and with her, quite soon, he would be reduced to an embarrassed incoherence.

12

They lived – Spenser and Laetitia Spender, who was known to the world as 'Lettuce' or 'Letty', much to her annoyance – in Chelsea. Although they had been married for several years, neither of them could have accounted for the length of their relationship – not even to each other. They had no children – this was Laetitia's choice. They rarely had sex – that was also her choice. 'Sex, Spenser,' she used to say, 'is not the same thing as love.' Since he had so little of the former, he was hardly in a position to judge. But they did indeed love each other; their relationship was close, based as it was upon a mutual inability to understand one another. They were like the survivors of a disaster who, by instinct, had forgotten what had happened to them.

It was clear to Laetitia that something was on Spenser's mind. When he got home he was humming tunelessly under his breath – a habit she detested – and he started immediately rearranging things, tidying the already tidy magazines, picking up imaginary pieces of fluff from the carpet.

'Where were you, little shrimp?' Laetitia had many such endearments for her husband, most of them on the diminutive side.

'I went out, actually, Letty.'

'I know you went out. Out is obvious. But where did you go, shrimpy?'

'I went back to the Scrubs, you know where the prison—'

'Yes, I know. What did you do that for?'

'I had this idea, Letty, actually.'

'Why didn't you do the shopping on the way, shrimpy? You know we need toilet paper.'

'I had this great idea, lettuce leaf.'

'Oh, yes.' Laetitia switched on the television, and three fire engines were to be seen hurtling over Tower Bridge. She momentarily lost interest in what she was saying. Anything to do with pursuit, or unpredictable violence, fascinated her.

'I'm going to start on a new film.'

'What kind of idea?'

'I said I'm going to start on a new film.'

'What kind of film?' She pulled her fingers through her

13

hair as she spoke, as if she were driving over Tower Bridge
herself and the wind was tearing at her.

'A film of *Little Dorrit*.'

'Little who?'

'*Little Dorrit*. It's the novel by Dickens. I'm going to turn it
into a film.'

She absorbed the knowledge while pretending not to, as
though she were on a diet and had quickly eaten a chocolate.
She smiled vacantly up at her husband.

'Well, that sounds a good idea. By the way, shrimpy, will
you look at my elbow for me. I think I've grazed it.'

He took her arm, gently, and inspected the spot with great
care. 'There's nothing there, Letty, nothing at all.'

It was no good, he knew it, they would have to go out to
eat – it would give him time to think. Also, it provided him
with an excuse to change his clothes. He always dressed to
think. A suit for formal, managerial thought – when per-
plexed over questions of finance, or a difficult colleague; a
sweater and jeans for informal thought, for thinking 'around'
a subject. He hovered in front of his wardrobe, examining the
mood of each garment. It would have to be a shirt-and-tie
night. He brushed his hair, looked at it in the large mirror on
one wall of the bedroom, and then brushed it in the opposite
direction; then he brushed it back again.

As they walked out into the King's Road, the old woman
passed them at the corner, pushing one pram ahead of her
and dragging one pram behind. She came this way often,
aiming with single-minded determination for a row of
wooden benches by the Royal Hospital. Her prams were
filled with scraps of old clothes and newspapers, empty tins of
Horlicks and old bottles stuffed with rags. She simply added
material to her piles; the stuff at the bottom of the prams
could not have been seen, or touched, for many years. It
represented the remnants of the Chelsea streets, perhaps the
only history they had.

She plodded along with a peculiarly benevolent expression, dressed in materials which closely resembled those in the
prams; she was like a tortoise between two shells. She would
have to be in it, he thought, or someone like her. 'It', the

14

project, had already taken on a confused but palpable life; like a watermark, it would now show on anything which Spenser held up to the light.

As he looked back over his shoulder, imagining the angle at which he would film her and the quality of light he might have used for this particular scene, Laetitia was imagining the speed with which she, too, could join the old woman on the streets of the city. It could all, she thought, be taken away, all of it, life, London, everything. It was a mystery how it all got started in the first place. She took Spenser's arm. 'I'm glad you've got a new project, shrimpy. It will give you something to do.'

'That's a tautology, Letty.'

'Is it? Anyway I'm glad it's a film and not another documentary.' As his wife talked, Spenser's eyes roved over the shop-fronts, the girls, the cars, never finding rest. 'It's going to mean a lot of work though, isn't it?'

'But work is important to me, Letty. You know that.' He was exasperated that she did not know him better. He pulled his shirt cuffs out from under his jacket with a punctilious gesture. 'First of all, I've got to find a backer. That's going to be a nightmare, actually.' He knew about the Film Finance Board, of course – that was always there. But he had never approached it for help. He claimed that it was a point of principle – which it was; but he was also scared of appearing as a supplicant.

'You'll do it, shrimp, you know you always do.'

Laetitia said this quite loudly, as they entered the restaurant, as if she were announcing the fact to the other diners there. The only advantage of the Edwardian Eatery was its relative cheapness. It was a place designed for tourists and, out of season, lapsed into a stunned incompetence. Old English agricultural implements had been stuck haphazardly upon the walls, and behind the cash register there was a large blown-up photograph of 'Derby Day 1911'. Next to that was an even larger photograph of two young children, shoeless, in ragged clothes, begging in the East End.

A waitress, wearing a tight-fitting dress with small lace frills all over it, handed Laetitia the tiny menu. The food was, like everything else, Old English – precooked and heated for convenience in a microwave oven.

15

'Shrimpy, what would you rather have, Edwardian stock-pot or roast beef? And, oh look, they've got your favourite, bread and butter pudding.'

Spenser felt trapped in this rising tide of false nostalgia; it was like being stuck within a set designed for an American television series. It was typical, anyway, of Chelsea – posturing, empty, with a kind of cheap bravura.

At first, Spenser and Laetitia talked sporadically over dinner. They knew each other too well to be interested in each other's attempts at conversation. When they talked, it was a game in which neither party wanted to embarrass the other by winning.

Spenser was drinking. He did not drink obsessively, but with a steady conviction. Almost any liquid would have done; the fact that it was cheap wine – and that he was getting drunk – was not immediately apparent to him. 'There's something strange about London, love...'— towards the end of the meal, Spenser's fitful conversation was gathering momentum, pushing relentlessly forward— 'That's why the Romans built their ruins here and everything. I'm sure there's something to it, some kind of magic or something. Did you know if you drew a line between all of Hawksmoor's churches, they would form a pentangle? Isn't that weird?'

Laetitia had assumed an expression of distant interest, nodding at Spenser and smiling while all the time trying to catch the waitress's eye; but the frills had disappeared behind a bust of Edward VII.

'You see, Lettuce, Dickens understood London. He was a great man, you know, he knew what it was all about. He knew that in a city people behave in different ways like, oh I don't know, like they were obsessed, Letty, are you listening to me? And he was here when it all started. He knew what was going to happen.'

Laetitia waved to the waitress, and wriggled her hand to signify 'bill'. Spenser, at the same moment, pointed at the empty wine bottle and smiled inanely. The waitress, with a little *moue* of her lips, decided to choose Spenser's gesture. Laetitia stared at her furiously.

'No one knows how a city works, oh go on, Letty, let's just have a little glass more, there was that Mumford woman I suppose wasn't there. But no one really knows what it's like. What has it done to me, or to you, Letty? What has it done to all the people in here?' He made a grand gesture towards the rest of the restaurant, and knocked over a wine glass, spilling part of its contents over the man sitting at the next table.

Job Penstone looked as if he was continually trying to live down to his name. A pale man, thin from nerves rather than physique, his eyes guarded by spectacles, his mouth by a pipe, he wore his middle age like a funeral cape. An air of exhaustion hovered above him: something within him had struggled and died.

While Spenser had been talking, Job had been surveying the restaurant and the blowsy, blown-up photographs of old festivals and street urchins. Those men and women all dead now, those children lingering in doorways, hungry, staring at the camera as though they might burrow within it and escape. He might set an essay on 'The Society of the Spectacle'.

Job Penstone was teaching a course in Victorian social history at a London polytechnic. When Spenser spilt the wine, it ran over a copy of Henry Mayhew's *London Labour and the London Poor* which Job had brought with him for comfort.

'I'm so sorry. I'm terribly sorry.' Spenser jumped up in his confusion, and knocked over the empty wine bottle. Laetitia set it down again upon the table with great deliberation. She wiggled her hand at the waitress again, with a terrible calm.

But Spenser had noticed the book now. There was a Victorian street scene upon the cover, rather like the photographs on the walls of the restaurant. 'That looks like an interesting thing to be reading. I'm sorry. I hope I haven't broken it, I mean ruined it.'

Job was alarmed by this sudden incursion into his world of speculation. 'No. That's all right . Sorry. That's fine. Really.'

'Sorry. This has something to do with the Victorians, or is that just the cover?'

'Yes. I mean no. It is about them.'

'Is that your interest?' Spenser rarely talked to strangers in this way, and his drunkenness gave his questions an intensity which he did not, in fact, feel.

'I teach a course in it, in them, sorry. For my sins.' Job

17

spoke with a fake cheeriness. He tried to smile at Laetitia, but the edges of his teeth showed disagreeably.

'I'm interested in them too, actually.'

'Oh yes?'

'I make films. Well, I used to make documentaries, and before that it was commercials, but now I'm making a film, well actually I hope to make a film of *Little*—'

'I'm sure the gentleman isn't interested in your whole career, Spenser, really.' She looked at Spenser with a mixture of anger and protectiveness, as if he were about to blurt out the secrets of his life and her own.

'I just want his advice, Letty.' He turned towards Job, and tapped the book as if it were a friendly animal. 'You are the exact person, the exact person, Mr—'

'Penstone. My name is Penstone.'

'You see, Mr Penstone, I'm making this film about *Little*—'

At this moment the waitress put down the bill. Laetitia clutched at it, and rose from her seat. 'I'm sorry about the mess, Mr Stone.' She took Spenser's arm, drew him upwards, smiled briefly at Job Penstone, and led Spenser away. She was too bored with him to speak. When they arrived back in the flat, Spenser wrote 'Penstone' on a packet of cigarettes and dropped it on the floor beside the bed.

That night, he dreamed that he could find no copy of *Little Dorrit* in the public library; he was walking home from a restaurant when Laetitia walked up beside him. She was carrying a copy of the novel, in white binding. He asked if he could borrow it from her, and she refused. He had a sudden sensation of intense anger. When he woke up, he knew that he had been crying. It was morning, but he returned to his sleep and dreamed of a planet of ghosts. Unlike Audrey, he would not remember his dream.

four

Rowan Phillips woke up with a start; he had dragged himself from the edge of a deep pit, only just in time to escape serious injury. His body seemed to be emitting faint shudders, like a generator running out of electricity. He had been drinking; he tried to hold on to his personality, which was trying to escape. *I must stop all this.* He wriggled his toes to see if there was any feeling in them. *I must stop drinking. Go back to Cambridge. Get on with the work.*

He was fully awake now, but less alert than when he had been asleep. Around his small bedroom were piles of papers and of books: *The London of Dickens, The World of Charles Dickens, Dickens in London: A Study in Structure, Dickens: The Baroque Lamp, The Burning Mirror: Charles Dickens, Hypothesis and Paradox in Dickens's London, Dickens and The Twisted Metastasis, The Flickering Flame: The Secret Dickens, Charles Dickens and Irony.* On and on they went, like registers of burials during a fatal epidemic.

Rowan Phillips, only thirty as he used to remind himself, was a tutor in English literature; the English faculty at Cambridge had now appointed him a lecturer. He was Canadian, and looked upon these academic awards with a mixture of transatlantic irony and colonial gratitude. He wrote books in the same way that other people doodle – compulsively, with little affection, defending himself against criticism by ignoring each work as soon as it was finished. He had published a novel which, begun as 'literary' fiction, had ended as a thriller. He had also published a short biography of Wilkie Collins, and was now involved in a critical study of Charles Dickens – a study, his publisher had told him, 'for the 1980s'.

Perhaps it was for Dickens's sake that he had bought a small flat in Gray's Inn Road – to be close to his 'material'.

But he doubted it. Rowan was a homosexual, and it was his fantasy that really lured him to the city. As he had been deprived of affection for most of his life, anonymous and, if possible, frequent sex seemed to him to be the ideal state. In London he could be free.

A man and woman were arguing in the flat next to his, in ferocious whispers. Rowan put his ear against the wall, but could hear nothing. He was fascinated by emotions in which he played no part. He tip-toed to the lavatory, from where the voices might be more audible, but still nothing. He decided to stay there, and contemplate the previous night. He had not 'had sex' – he said the words out loud, testing them for their weight and worth. It seemed to him an eminently valuable phrase – 'sex', like 'work', its own glittering reward. It had not always been like that. His triumphant progress as a young academic had meant, at first, that he had had to carry repression and frustration aloft, above his head, like gold insignia.

His appointment as tutor had unleashed the first wave; success encouraged a certain relaxation. Before, he had said, 'I am not interested in sex', and his face had become thin, his breath turned sour. Now, he said, 'I am a homosexual. What shall I do?' He visited a psychiatrist who assured him that his homosexuality – or gayness, as it was still often called by older people – was something which needed exploring and encouraging; a 'supportive relationship' was suggested. He left the man dissatisfied; he had wanted to reveal himself to someone – anyone – as possessing a profoundly tortured personality. And he was handed a do-it-yourself kit, and told to get to work.

And so he had. 'Have sex' – the words might have been engraved on stone. Rowan Phillips searched for sex assiduously in London; he saw the city as a sea from which some god might rise but, in the meantime, he was quite happy to drown in its waters. He visited pubs and public lavatories; he followed strangers down dark alleys; he became infatuated with any handsome man who smiled upon him. He masturbated as often as he could, conjuring up fantasies which spread a lurid glow through his waking hours. Already, while on the lavatory, he had an erection. The argument in the next flat was still going on. He flattened his ear against the wall: nothing definite. He decided to masturbate.

The only way to rescue himself from the day, he thought as he did so, was to be decisive, do some kind of work. He would go back to Dickens. He would take a trip across the river, and find the old sites by Southwark. He might even pick somebody up. Just as he was about to come, the telephone rang. A male voice asked for Rowan. He knew at once who it was: a boy whom he had slept with, and who had asked for his number afterwards. In a fit of absent-minded benevolence, Rowan had given it to him. 'Hello? Is that you, Rowan?' Rowan adopted an English accent, always useful in an emergency of this kind. 'No. Sorry. You have the wrong number, I'm afraid.' 'Oh I see, sorry to bother you.' The boy, whose name Rowan could not remember, let the words out in a rush as though he had been unexpectedly punched. Rowan put down the receiver. Free in one bound.

He felt the same sense of liberation on the top deck of the bus; nothing could touch him here. The image of a time capsule was one which returned to him in such situations: he was a traveller, omniscient, untouched by what he sees or hears, watching climactic struggles pass by as if they were small boats upon the water. The people outside this bus were transient things, their expressions as delicate and as impersonal as flowers growing beneath a jar. Only the buildings seemed solid, lasting; they formed one building in his imagination – brown, squat, filled with smoke.

He was falling into a doze when a middle-aged woman, smelling strongly of stale food, sat next to him, lowering herself into the seat with a kind of defiant certainty. She began talking – was it into the air, or was it directed at him? 'That war was terrible it was really, a million killed and all for a shilling a day. My face got poisoned from it, all the neighbours were looking from the windows and that dog was killed. Have you got a dog?' Her voice sounded too young for the body, as if a record were being played too fast. She was peering at him, but not seeing him. 'No.' He stared out of the window, his hand clenched around the notebook in his pocket. She poked through an old plastic shopping bag. 'I don't care who knows about the mess he made on me I could have chucked him off the top here and got rid of the poison, and millions died millions of them all of them germs.'

He wanted desperately to get off the bus, but his panic had drained him of any strength he might have had to push past her. He might have been made of paper, or transparent plastic. 'All they want is my cunt you could have put a hand on it in them days and felt nothing, and then I made them shut their traps.' She seemed to recollect herself for an instant, and stared ahead in silence. And then, as defiantly and as abruptly as she had arrived, she got up from her seat and scurried down the stairs.

Rowan sat back in a daze of relief, as if he had been spared some terrible physical harm. His mind was blank, he could raise nothing from it. He was still clenching the notebook, when, some minutes later, he saw the street signs and knew that it was here he must alight. The place itself was nondescript. Some small shops, a supermarket, a book-maker's, two or three pubs, and some tenement blocks which stretched into the middle distance. Two children passed by Rowan on skateboards. Cigarette packets and old newspapers had been discarded in the already crowded gutters; scraps of old front pages, like fragments of conversation, had been blown together. CHINA ATOM SCARE, AMERICA AC-CUSES, SOVIET THREAT....

He was approached by a young tramp. There were several of them, sitting by the entrance to Borough Tube Station like clowns abandoned by a travelling circus. 'Got some change, sir, just to see me on my way?' The young man's eyes were curiously placid and yielding; the voice that of someone simply asking for what was, after all, no more than his due. The other tramps looked on with impersonal curiosity. Rowan Phillips disliked confrontation of any kind, even the dim prospect of argument or unpleasantness. He found a silver coin in his pocket and gave it to the young man, with a smile which, he hoped, mixed altruism with friendliness. But he would not have dared ask him, with his torn but brightly coloured clothes and his carrot-red hair, what he most wanted to know – where Marshalsea prison, one of the objects of his quest, had once been. It might seem too obvious a provocation.

The tramps watched him as he walked away, and started muttering amongst themselves. He saw St George's Church just ahead of him – that, at least, was still recognisable. Rowan Phillips walked quickly up its steps and tried the door, but it was locked. It was here that Little Dorrit had once sought refuge – the door had been locked then, also – but where was the site of the old prison itself?

He walked down the high street a little, passed a garage, a pub, a supermarket. He walked into a small shop where, thinking of his breath, he bought some peppermints. An old Indian woman stared at him, with the eyes of a dead owl. 'Do you happen to know where the old Marshalsea prison is?' She kept on staring. 'I guess you don't. Thanks.' On the street outside, an old man, with a cigarette hanging out of his mouth, was selling the evening newspaper. He was wearing an antique 'flat cap' which rivalled its owner in the number of its creases and its general, battered shape. 'Excuse me, can you tell me where the old Marshalsea prison used to be?' 'You what, mate?' 'Do you know the old Marshalsea prison? Famous old place?' He shook his head, or rather his cap, in a ruminative fashion. 'No. Marshalsea prison.' He paused for thought. 'As in Marshalsea Road. But it ain't there. I can't help you in that direction, not to my knowledge. I can't place that.' He paused again. 'The only prison I know is down Brixton way. Is that any good to you?' 'Yes, I'll try that. Good of you to help. I'll try.' And Rowan Phillips adopted his most cheerful air, as though Brixton prison were exactly the place he was planning to spend the day.

Timothy Coleman was walking, in the opposite direction, down the same street. He had finished an early shift and was just returning from the municipal swimming baths, his towel under his arm, his hair sleeked back and still dark with the water. He resembled some creature of the sea.

This was, at least, how he seemed to Rowan Phillips. He saw Tim walking easily towards him, and was unable to take his eyes from him. This was it. This was the boy. He had imagined the same thing many times before, but each time was always the first time. Tim was thinking of Audrey; he was least aware of himself as a person at exactly that moment when Rowan was most aware of him. Tim was, from the start, placed at a disadvantage; as though Rowan were filling some emptiness in Tim's own sense of himself.

As they drew closer, Tim was aware that he was being looked at and, as a result, decided to look up at the sky, and examine it for signs of weather. Rowan, however, was less modest. He decided to use a broad Canadian accent, the kind which his characters had used in his novel. 'Say, can you tell me where the old Marshalsea prison might be. I was told it might be around here.' He might have been a tourist, passionless and lost. Timothy moved back a step, to take in this message and inspect its bearer. 'I'm sorry, mate. What was that?'

'I'm looking for the old prison. I have a hunch it's someplace around here. Is that right?'

'Oh, right. Right. Hang on a tick. I was told.' Tim had a slight nervous twitch in his cheek when surprised or embarrassed; he put a hand to his face in order to hide it. Audrey had been talking about that prison. It was only a few hundred yards from where she worked – hadn't she said that? He stroked his face, as if calming it. Somewhere down here, on the left, isn't that it?

'Hold on a sec, mate. Just walk this way a bit.' He walked alongside Rowan, his hand reaching spasmodically for his face, scrutinising the walls and side-streets for a sign. Rowan was surreptitiously smelling his breath in the cupped palms of his hands. He popped a peppermint in his mouth. He was in a perplexity of feeling – relieved that he might find the place after all, excited by the closeness of the handsome young man, frustrated at the prospect of soon losing him.

'Do you live around here? In this neighbourhood?'

'Not far, really. I should know this prison place like I know my own sister, but I just can't place it yet. I can't place it.' They walked a few yards in silence, a little apart. Tim saw Tabard Street, and some childhood memory stirred him.

'This might be it, mate. Let's just cut along here and have a butchers.'

And there it was, down Tabard Street on the left. A small open space, with two or three benches in the middle; it was surrounded by large tower-blocks, so that it resembled a small wound which had never healed; a brisk wind sent dead leaves revolving over the paths. A blue metal notice had been fixed upon one wall: 'This site was originally the MARSHALSEA PRISON made famous by the late CHARLES DICKENS in his well known work "Little Dorrit". The prison was destroyed by fire on December 14 1885.'

Fancy it being so close, Tim thought, and me never remembering it. Rowan walked up to the metal placard. It was hanging precariously now, since the wall was crumbling around it. One column of ants moved down the old stones, and another moved up. They did not pause.

'Yes, this is it.' Rowan turned back to Tim. 'Do you know this area? I guess you do. You know, I'm writing a book about it, this old part of London I mean—' he chose a half-lie.

'Oh yeah? Is that right?'

'You seem to know your way around here.'

'I suppose I do. In a way, like.' As Tim turned towards Rowan, he tripped and half-fell upon the gravel path. Rowan bent over him and, hesitantly, took him by the arm and helped him up.

'Are you okay?'

'I'm fine, thanks. Just a stumble, like.' Tim brushed pieces of gravel off his trousers, and looked studiously again at the blue plaque.

'I don't suppose,' Rowan said quickly, taking advantage of this sudden intimacy, 'that you would give me a tour?'

Tim was embarrassed but also impressed, meeting a writer just off the cuff like that, after a swim. He was thinking of Audrey. Audrey would love to meet a writer. He knew that he could not himself still her restlessness – he was not large enough for that. To present a writer to her, as his friend, might add a certain substance to him; it was almost as good as handing her a small cheque from the pools.

'My girl-friend knows everything around here. Audrey. She knows all there is to know, really.' He thought he noticed a slight change of expression on Rowan's face, as though his smile had dissolved at the corners. 'She could give you a hand, like.'

'Are you sure?' Rowan was disappointed, caught now in a situation which he had created. 'And she won't mind?'

'She likes to help, she does really.'

It would have been quite impossible for Tim to reply in any other way. He was temperamentally inclined to please others, and he placed this aura of benevolence, like a yoke, over everyone he knew. The wind now had grown chill, and the quietness of twilight fell upon the site of the old prison. And so it was that Timothy Coleman and Rowan Phillips fell in with each other.

five

That next morning, after the drunken dinner with Laetitia, a plan had already formulated itself in Spenser Spender's mind. He had placed it there even as he slept. He would proceed methodically. His first step was to take the cigarette packet, with the name Penstone scrawled upon it, and put it carefully in a drawer. Now he would telephone the 'creative director' of the last film company he had worked for – 'creative', in such circles, being an adjective constantly in search of a noun. If that didn't work, he would try the English extension of certain Los Angeles film companies. Such extensions had proliferated recently, and it was now often easier to make a film in London than it was in Hollywood. If they were of no help, he would try the Film Finance Board, or a private backer. Although the track ahead of him was full of hurdles, he would pretend for the time being that he was travelling across flat ground.

He dialled the number of the 'creative director', Iain St John Smart. The line did not connect. He tried again; a 'phone rang somewhere. Spenser Spender could hear its echo, and then it broke off. The third time was successful. 'Hello, Iain?'

'Yes.'

'This is Spenser Spender, Iain.'

The 'phone erupted like a geiger counter in the presence of a radiation leak. 'Spenser, old son, how lovely to hear from you. Long time and no see and so on. That thing you did on the box was magnificent, just magnifico. I was just thinking of you this morning, if only I had got my hands on that, there is no knowing, no knowing, old son, what we might have done with it.'

'I do have something which might interest you, actually.'

'Oh yes?' The tone was subtly modulated to one of guarded sympathy.

'An extension of the television piece, actually.'

'I'm interested already, Spenser, I'm interested. Very simpatico on that one.'

'Can't we have lunch together?'

'Much as I would love to, old thing, lunch is out for a couple of weeks. Time's winged horses and so on.'

Spenser Spender decided to use the 'old thing' approach himself.

'Oh come on, Iain, you can spare me a few minutes in your office if nothing else. You won't be wasting your time, you know, actually.'

There was a pause, as if Iain were measuring that commodity on a pocket calculator.

'Oh well, you win, Spenser, you win. Why don't you call round today around midday? Byeee.'

The offices of Star International were in Wardour Street; they resembled, superficially at least, the amusement arcades which surrounded them: the same lights around the large windows, and similar posters proclaiming 'coming attractions'. The people both in the offices and the arcades behaved in much the same way, also: a show of uninterest when working the machines, and feigned indifference to either success or failure. There was always another machine, another project, waiting to be switched on. The last film Spenser Spender had made with Star International had been a twenty-minute 'short', about the making of a television commercial. All the loathing which Spenser Spender felt for that particular form, and his own involvement in it, had been poured into the film. As a consequence, it had been a success. Spenser Spender was an interesting property as far as Iain St John Smart was concerned – not vital, or particularly important, just interesting.

When Spenser Spender was shown into his brightly coloured office, St John Smart was gazing out of his smoked, double-glazed windows; the world outside had become a silent film. He turned, beamed, put out his hand, walked over, had Spenser Spender in a modern and uncomfortable chair, lit a cigarette, sat down, cupped a hand over his chin, and waited, beaming. He exuded an air of not being interested in preliminary civilities.

'How's the old lady?'

'She's fine, Iain, thanks.'

'That's good. That's just fine.' Iain shifted impatiently in his chair.

'My idea is a perfectly simple one, actually, Iain.'

'Faint heart never won fair and so on. Go on, old son.'

'Do you remember when the British Theatre performed those Dickens novels, over a few months?'

'Remember? It was incredibly exciting. Enthralling. I really mean it.'

'Do you remember the tremendous response as well, actually?'

'Do I just.'

'Well, I want to go to the next stage. I want to film *Little Dorrit*.'

'Little what?'

'*Little Dorrit*, actually. It's that one about the girl in the prison. Don't you remember, at the British Theatre?'

'Like yesterday.'

'I see something around two hours, filmed on location in London, all abbreviated from the book naturally. And an entirely unknown cast.'

'Naturally.'

'I don't foresee a more than average budget. I would estimate nine months shooting, three months editing. I think we might hit upon a nerve, actually.'

'Spenser Spender, you have done it again, old thing, you really have. You have lit a flame in me that will not die.' He put out his cigarette. 'You may definitely be on to something here.' Iain St John Smart's expression, in which the smile curled like a piece of stale bread, had not altered but his eyes were quite calm and cold. He laid out a row of brightly coloured pills on his desk as his secretary, on cue, brought in a glass of water.

'But let's just lay out the problems in front of us, old chum. One. On a literary thing like this we're not going to get American distribution without a fight. Excuse me.' He swallowed the first of the pills, but the smile held. 'Two.

Excuse me.' Another gulp. 'No stars means problems for our publicity boys. Now, you know and I know that they do fuck-all, but the old boys on the board listen to them, you see, old thing. That's the sticker there.' He motioned upwards, as if to the sky. 'And then third. Location shooting in London. Excuse me. Is getting tricky. There are problems, old son, there are problems. My cup runneth over, as they say in the bible.'

Beyond the smoky texture of the glazed windows, the sky over Soho was darkening, and the first few drops of rain began to fall.

'But think about it, Iain. Think of this as just a preliminary chat, actually. I'll get the details down on paper and send them to you.'

'I think you should do that, Spenser, you should definitely do that. We're going to keep in close touch on this one.'

'Can I take it that you're interested, then?'

'You can indeed, Spenser. I want you to keep working on it.'

Iain St John Smart was out from behind his desk, hand outstretched, beaming still, hand shaken, Spenser led to the door, waved at as he walked disconsolately down the corridor.

When he left Star Enterprises and walked into Wardour Street, regretting that for once he had relied upon enthusiasm rather than careful preparation, the rain was falling heavily upon Soho. The windows of the arcades and shops were streaked with dirty water; the gutters were already flowing, coming to life. Iain St John Smart was watching Spenser Spender from behind his double-glazed windows; he was trying to remember the name of that book he had mentioned.

Sheet lightning took up the whole sky, and the rain now seemed to leap upward from the pavement and rise to the clouds again. Spenser Spender ran for shelter, towards the nearest pub, when he saw Pally again. He was sitting on a bench beside the pub; his face was illuminated by the lightning and he stared up at it, his hair and clothes sodden. 'Come on, Pally, come on inside,' Spenser Spender yelled. A gust of wind blew rain into his face, and his vision was blurred for an instant. 'Come on, Pally, don't you remember me?' But Pally, somehow, had gone. The bench was empty.

six

Rowan Phillips and Timothy Coleman walked together down Marshalsea Road. They were like two species of birds who had by accident decided upon the same route – Tim taking rather larger strides, like a flamingo, Rowan walking quickly beside him, like a mud warbler with the wind behind it. As the twilight settled over them, they talked about this area of the great city, how it was that so many old things lay here, and how many had remained unknown or neglected. Only last year the ruins of a Roman temple had been discovered on a building site by the new post office building. That's where Audrey works. It's funny, but she was mentioning that Marshalsea place.

And Rowan told Tim of the scene when Little Dorrit and Little Mother, locked out of the Marshalsea prison, had walked up and down Borough High Street all night, had crossed London Bridge, of the crazed woman who had whispered to them and of the strange, secretive men who whistled on street corners and told each other to 'mind the women'. Tim listened intently but saw such things as what they were: stories, fairy tales, not connected with the reality of any place.

When they reached Audrey's block of flats, looking a dismal grey in the twilight, Tim asked Rowan to wait downstairs in the hall for a tick, just to make sure if she was decent. But really, he meant, to explain and if necessary to apologise.

Audrey had been living last night's dream for most of the day; she imagined herself the neglected child of a rich father, now down on his luck. She had done her hair in what she thought to be an appropriately plain style before setting off for work, and had worn one of her older dresses. The day's work had also tired her and now she sat, watching a fly as it

31

buzzed idly around her sitting room. It was late, she thought, for a fly, October, when Tim rang her bell. His explanation was awkward, but brief.

'You've never brought him back here, then, have you?' Yes, Tim acknowledged that he had.

'But he's a writer, Aud, and you know how you like your books.'

'Yes, but I never said to bring one back with you, did I?' She was thinking, and look at the state of this place anyway. 'Well, go on then. Drag him up. We can't have him loitering down there all night.'

Rowan Phillips was uncomfortable. He was pretending to these people that he was writing a book about their area; he was, in fact, behaving like a confidence trickster, prying into their lives. In addition, he might get saddled with some boring woman. In a certain sense, he enjoyed his novel situation – it was as if he had become a voyeur – but he wanted at all costs not to become involved, to leave himself too open to discovery and possible embarrassment. He allowed himself to be led up the old, stone stairs.

'This is Mr Phillips, Audrey, he's a writer.'

'Oh, a writer. Well, that is nice.'

He was asked to make himself comfortable, not to stand upon ceremony.

'Well, this must be an interesting area for you, Mr Phillips. There's a lot of history around here.'

'Yes, I guess there is.'

Audrey glanced at herself in a small mirror on the wall. There was an absence of books in the room, she thought. She would have to make up for them somehow.

'I'm sorry this place is in such a state, Mr Phillips, but we weren't expecting company, not off the cuff you might say. I wasn't always so poor, mind you. There was money in my family once upon a time. Oh yes.' This last remark seemed to be directed towards Tim, who was looking at Audrey in a state of some astonishment. Rowan Phillips smiled and nodded.

'Yes, there was money all right, but my father lost it in the fifties. That was a terrible time for us, a terrible time. We never recovered after that and so I said to my father, I said don't you worry your head over me. I can make my own way. I wanted to be a writer too, you know, but what with one thing and another I never got round to it. I ended up at the post office, did Tim tell you about that, but I read a lot still and if it's history you want to know I can tell you, Mr Phillips.' Rowan glanced at Tim, not knowing quite what to make of these revelations so suddenly vouchsafed. The boy's face expressed perplexity mixed with a concern so palpable that his whole body seemed to be reaching towards Audrey.

'We found the site of that Marshalsea place, Aud, just where you said it was.' Audrey took this in, graciously, but did not look at Tim. 'I've been thinking about that prison and all the poor souls who passed through there, Mr Phillips. There has been so much suffering and distress around here, there really has. It makes me sick to think about it. I don't know what your politics are, Mr Phillips, but when you think of how this government is treating the poor and the unemployed, it can't really be all that different now from what it was then, can it? All those young boys begging down by the station – wasn't that a Victorian thing, too, all that? Begging and all?' Audrey had worked herself into an agony of words, and stood up. The fly was buzzing around her now, seeming to swoop at her. She brushed it away, and smoothed her dress.

They sat for a moment in silence. Tim tried to rescue Audrey by talking about Rowan's book, but he faltered and fell silent. Rowan began talking about Little Dorrit, the prison, the old church. Audrey gazed at him in astonishment, as if summoning her strength for one more effort. She told him of her dream, of being inside that same prison, worrying about money. And wasn't it the oddest thing, she had never heard of this Little Dorrit person. Strange really, wasn't it?

Yes, it was most peculiar, Rowan supposed. Tim nodded in agreement, but the pain was so clear upon his face it was like that of a small animal caught in a hunter's trap. Rowan looked at him. He could look at him forever. But perhaps under more propitious circumstances. He glanced at his watch, just long enough for Audrey to notice.

'It's funny that you should have met Tim like this, Mr Phillips. Quite a coincidence really, what with the dream and all. I hope we haven't disappointed you with our natterings and one thing and another. And you will come again, won't you, I've got a lot of history stored away up here.' She touched her head as though it was an independent entity, purely there for his convenience. Rowan said that he would like that, he really would. Tim smiled, but the smile stuck upon his face. He felt that he had betrayed them both, Audrey and Mr Phillips. Rowan rose to leave. Audrey had decided that she would like to show him round, let him have a gander, at the area. He made an elaborate point of writing down her telephone number; he also, with a suggestion of casualness, took down that of Tim.

He walked out into the street, in a state of confused triumph. He had carried it off. The girl talked too much, of course, but now he had Timothy's telephone number. As he walked down towards the bus stop, he saw the young tramp with the carrot-red hair, shouting and screaming on a corner. It seemed impossible that such mildness had turned to ferocity, that the docility had become anger. 'I'm thirsty,' he was screaming, 'I'm fucking thirsty!' Rowan Phillips hurried on.

seven

After his unfortunate and, he knew, fruitless interview with Iain St John Smart, Spenser Spender had gone back to *Little Dorrit* in order to draw what confidence and inspiration he could from it. He went through the novel carefully now, making notes as he did so, in order to devise a scenario. He would remove all elements in the novel which took place outside London. He would, in fact, end the film at the close of the first book when the Dorrits, after the unexpected discovery of their fortune, are let out of the debtors' prison. It would close with Arthur Clennam carrying Little Dorrit over the portal of the Marshalsea, after she had fallen into a dead faint at the thought of the weary vacancy, the purposelessness, of her new freedom.

Several images and sequences had already formed themselves in his mind. There would be the Clennam home near London Bridge, shadowy, blackened with an accumulation of pride and repressed guilt. He could see the house clearly, looming out of the darkness and yet a part of it, like a fantasy of the imperious will. There would be the yard of the Marshalsea itself, with Mr Dorrit the willing accomplice in his own servitude, battening on the lives of others in order to strengthen the walls of his own misery and abasement. These sequences, Spenser Spender had already decided, would have to be filmed within the prison he had used before. He knew it. It was real, it was solid: the film needed a strong charge of contemporaneity.

And there would be the scene when Little Dorrit, with her half-witted companion Little Mother, walked all night by the Thames, surrounded by the dangerous and the deranged from whom they fear no harm. There would be scenes in Bleeding Heart Yard, where the poor of London lived crowded together, and in Hampton Court, where the dilapidated

35

remnants of aristocratic families were similarly crowded and lost. The film would be dark – perhaps in black and white? It would suggest an air of close confinement and decay but it would be, paradoxically, the only air which these poor souls could breathe. They were linked in their common destiny, and from it derived solace in the face of that unknowable 'freedom' of which they were all, secretly, afraid. He roughed out a shooting schedule, and estimated the approximate costs.

With this material, he approached film and television companies. Young men in dark suits, and slightly older men in faded denim jeans, were enthusiastic, dazzled by the 'concept'. They wanted to work with him on this one, it could be really big. They would discuss it with the big white chiefs upstairs. From some he would then hear no more; from others would come a summons for a second meeting. The young men were polite now, sympathetic, really distraught at what they were letting through their fingers – but, of course, Spenser, there are bigger fish in the sea than us, you know – but they had these union problems, and there was this nightmarish production back-log, and they had this budgetary manager going bananas back at head office. They would have another go, of course, but they wished him the best of luck elsewhere – just to be on the safe side, old chap.

After one such meeting, Spenser Spender walked slowly back by the South Bank. It was evening now, and he stopped for a drink in a cafeteria by the river. He sat among people whom he had never seen before, whose destinies were strange to him. A middle-aged woman was with a young boy, probably her son. She was highly animated, acting out episodes from their own private store of memories, and the little boy laughed and clapped. When they stood up to go, Spenser Spender noticed that the boy was emaciated, as if wasted by some disease, and that he walked with a pronounced stoop. His mother followed him out, both protecting him, and propelling him forward, with her hands; he was still laughing. For once, Spenser Spender had a sense of other people's lives – of a different set of constrictions, of other and more difficult circumstances than his own. And yet his life was linked with theirs, and all who had preceded or would follow them.

He left the café and walked beside the Thames. The river was still, as though gathering to itself the white and orange beams of the street lamps which were reflected in its darkness. On the steps of Charing Cross Bridge, a flautist was playing with an air of gentle vacancy. The sounds of the flute crept over the bridge, and seemed to dance over the heads of the men and women who were walking above the river. Spenser Spender was filled with a sensation of lightness, as though his own body were moving out, too, across the water, implicated in the lives of these human beings who trudged slowly through the dark. And they, also, became part of him – as though he contained them all within himself at the same time as they directed him forward. The pattern was one, within and without. Each human figure seemed to emit its own brightness, so that the bridge itself resembled a line of energy, and one of irresistible momentum and sweetness. Spenser Spender was too elated to reflect then upon this experience; but he knew that it would remain with him, if he took care to nourish it.

eight

The air was warm for October, Audrey thought, as she crossed Charing Cross Bridge. She heard the music, and slowed down her step in order to hear it longer. Funny, really, that you don't get more flutes out on a night like this. They brighten everything up a bit.

She was on her way to a seance, on the suggestion of her friend at work, Margery, who dabbled. 'There's a first time for everything,' Audrey had explained to Tim, 'and Margery swears by it. Anyway I'm just going for a laugh.' He greeted the news with resignation. Audrey's ups and downs, as she referred to them, were becoming more and more frequent and, like the acceleration of strobe lighting, they were beginning to conceal from Timothy the object of his love. He accepted her new enthusiasm as an exile accepts another milestone on the road leading from home.

The seance was to be held near Ealing Common, in the house of Miss Norman, clairvoyant and spiritual counsellor. She was well-known in mediumistic circles for her pragmatic approach to the spirit world, which she tended to address as if she were a customer in Harrods. She was peremptory with her requests, annoyed on the rare occasions she was kept waiting.

Audrey and Margery were ushered into Miss Norman's waiting room, her vestibule of the spirit world, as the sound of yapping dogs reached them from an upper floor. Margery was a little nervous; she sat, hunched up in a white raincoat, on a small and uncomfortable chair, waiting for the summons. Audrey widened her eyes with her fingers, and made low moaning noises.

'Oh shut up, Aud, she'll be in any minute.'

'Ohhhh I'm coming for you, Margery Fisher.'

'Honestly, Audrey, act your age, you daft haporth.'

Their conversation was interrupted by the entry of another

member of the circle. A young man, with extremely long hair and a small beard, seemed to walk in sideways like a crab, keeping his eyes upon the carpet. He smiled to himself from time to time, but paid no attention to Audrey or Margery. He was followed by a middle-aged couple who looked, and sounded, as if they were on a coach-outing to see a new play.

'Is this your first time then, love?' the male component of the couple asked Audrey. 'You'll enjoy it, you know, it's a whole new world up there.' He took out a large white handkerchief and blew his nose very loudly. The young man laughed briefly, and slid his eyes toward the wallpaper.

It was fortunate, perhaps, that Miss Norman should enter at this moment, hurriedly, in a flurry of business-like activity, the secretary to the stars. She gave Audrey a quick, business-like glance. 'So this is our new face, is it? I hope you haven't come expecting miracles, dear. I don't deal in miracles here. It'll be £10, payable as you leave.' There was a slight bulge in her throat, which oscillated in a determined fashion. 'But you have a good aura, dear, I'll say that for you. Be careful with the legs, though, they may cause trouble in years to come.' She surveyed the others rapidly. 'Well, let's be having you next door.'

'Next door' was the room for the seance. A square table, with the flaps down, had been placed in the centre; there were six chairs around it. A large candle, lodged uneasily in a floral saucer, had been placed in the middle. Audrey felt funny, she was to say later, as soon as she sat herself down. She felt sort of tingly. Miss Norman sat at one end, like a company secretary at a board meeting. 'We have a new presence with us tonight, friends,' she announced, 'a new member of our circle.' They bowed their heads, as if saying grace before some lavish meal. 'This new soul who has sought us out, friends, lend her your strength.' Miss Norman beat out a staccato rhythm on the table, and the others joined in. After a pause, they held hands, and Miss Norman leaned across the table and blew out the candle. The sour-smelling smoke rose upward.

It was then that Audrey passed out. She remembered later only a flash of light, as though a lamp had been turned on inside her head. She became rigid, her back arched forward.

Margery looked at her in distaste, assuming that she was putting on some kind of performance. The others kept their heads bowed. And then Margery's distaste turned to astonishment when a clear, small voice issued from Audrey's mouth in the way that the sound of a fly might emerge from a wooden box.

'I am so little but I was born here.'

Miss Norman, quite used to such revelations, looked at Audrey with a vague interest, as one might look at a stranger who has wandered into a party. 'Who are you, dear?'

'It is the first night I have ever been away from home. I hope there is no harm in it.' The voice had a certain lightness to it, like that of a child or a mad woman. Margery felt quite dizzy and confused. She was worried that her hands were getting sweaty, locked as they were in the grip of the young man.

'Tell us your name, dear, and all about yourself.'

'Where do I come from and where do I go to? London is so large, so barren and so wild.'

'Yes, I know, dear. Tell us a bit more about yourself.'

'Why, sir, I am the child of this place.'

'A little bit more, love. We're interested. We want to help.'

'Little Dorrit. I am the child of the Marshalsea.'

nine

Little Arthur sits in his room and stares at his little love on the wall. He feels quite calm, now that it is all over. His palace is closed; he has no machines to guard, since they were taken away in a lorry. It is as if those years had never been. 'We'll be fine and dandy now,' he tells his little comfort, the photograph shining on the wall, 'we'll be as snug as two peas in a poddy-pod-pod.' He puts the kettle on, and slices two pieces of bread for toast. He is neat and economical in all of his movements.

He hauls himself on to the table by the window, and stares down at the gardens. Rubbish is burning in one of them, the smoke and the heat make the air quiver in front of Little Arthur. Who is that child in the garden there? Surely it isn't his little girl? It must be, with that light step, and the fair hair tied back. But how has she got out of the nest and downstairs without his knowing about it? She is a little devil of a sweet, and no mistake. He will have to go and fetch her back before she does herself a mischief, down there with them. He runs down the stairs, swinging himself off the bottom step. He opens the front door carefully, so as not to frighten her, and scurries out into the street.

He walks quickly towards the gardens – there she is, my little darling, my little caterpillar, playing by herself. 'Hey, little lovely,' he calls softly to her, 'come on home now.' The girl knows Little Arthur by sight, as all the children in this neighbourhood do, and she is not frightened by him.

'I am home,' she tells him. 'This is our garden.'

He is annoyed at her for not telling the truth, and squeezes through the ramshackle fence. 'No, my little pea, this isn't our garden. This is where they live. You belong with me, nice and cosy.' The child gazes at him. She does not know the rules of this game.

'Come on, sheep. Let's skip along home now.' He walks towards her, his arms open, his large hands clawing the air. She retreats a little more and stares at him. 'Don't run, sweet pea, you know I love you dearest.'

The girl runs off now towards her back door, and calls over her shoulder. 'Get away, short-arse!' This is what the children call Little Arthur. He has heard it before. Now he stares at the retreating figure of the little girl as astounded as if it were his own shadow leaping away from him.

Little Arthur knows that she has been taken by them; perhaps she is drugged or had her brains washed. This is their plan, of course, to turn her into one of them as soon as the machines were gone. He is frozen by the knowledge. He might as well be dead and buried. He holds his hands above his head, but his fists now are clenched. He stands immobile in this posture, like a child's drawing of rage.

There are two or three faces peering at him now – he can see them without looking, he has always seen them. He leaves the gardens grimacing at the faces, and climbs back up the stairs to his room. He is panting now. The water has boiled out of the kettle and is making an odd, throttled sound. The bread is lying next to the knife, ready for toasting. Little Arthur turns off the electric ring, and sits upon the table.

His mind is as blank as the sky at which he gazes; slowly, the morning light changes into the more gentle light of the afternoon and is reflected, too, upon his upturned face. The photograph of his little blossom, still shining with varnish, smiles upon him and gives him strength. But they have taken her away. Everything has been taken away. He slides off the table and walks in a circle, in the middle of the room, speeding up so that now he is running around with his fists clenched again. He comes to a decision. He will make a point of saving her – make a point of it. All that innocence cannot go to pot. He will take the bread-knife with him, just in case of conversation.

He walks slowly now, down the green-painted corridor which smells of boiled potatoes and custard, down the stairs, and out into the high street. Later, people will remember seeing Little Arthur pass, glaring into shop windows as though angry at his own reflection. But he does not see himself – he leaves that to them – he is watching them inside their shops and offices, always busy, busy, busy. What is their world compared to his nest with his love?

He turns the corner of Tabard Street and there, oh great joy, can it be, is his pea-blossom. Returned. Safe. She has wriggled away from them. Now they are together. 'Little pea, I am here for you. I have come for you!' The little girl turns around and lets out a sharp, squeaking noise, like chalk being scraped across a blackboard. Little Arthur rushes towards her, as if she has been hurt, and his knife falls out of his pocket with a clatter but he does not hear it. The girl runs into the small park at the end of the street. 'That isn't the way home, little angel, is it?' He rushes after her into the park. She stands silent upon the gravel path. Her eyes are wide now.

'Come on now, don't play baby games with your Arthur. I'll put the kettle on.' He takes her by the arm, his large hands gently touching the frail body; she shakes him off silently, but stands there still. 'Come on, pet of my life, time is running away with us. We must leave here before they come.' She starts to cry, and Little Arthur peers round to see if there is a face or two about. No. Not yet. They haven't discovered that she has escaped. 'You were a good angel to get away, a good angel.'

She begins to moan now, higher and higher until it almost reaches a scream, and Little Arthur puts his large hand over her mouth, her throat, to stop her. 'Please, dove, don't do it, don't do it. You'll attract faces, my dove, please don't.' He holds her tighter now, sensing his own panic as well as hers. He is back in the Fun Palace looking at the letter, he is eight years old again with the knowledge that he will not grow, he is weeping again at last.

The little girl has stopped moaning, her eyes open and staring, it seems, at the blue plaque upon the wall. 'Can you read now, angel? I have books at home for us, and we'll burrow ourselves in them, won't we?' But she does not answer and, laughing at the good times they will have together, he lays her body gently upon the gravel path. They will come after us now but we will laugh last, won't we, little love, we will laugh last.

But the little love is silent.

This was how they found Little Arthur and his only love, beneath a blue plaque in a small park, the love dead and Little Arthur looking at them, unabashed, for the first time.

ten

Laetitia Spender sometimes thought that, if she closed her eyes for long enough, she might cease to exist, she might discover her vanishing point. Her reality, she was convinced, was known only to herself; for everyone else she was Spenser Spender's wife, very attractive, really, hadn't she been a model once? She hated being called 'Lettuce' or even Letty: it confirmed her status merely as an object. But somehow the names had stuck – perhaps she did resemble an abbreviation or a vegetable. At these moments, she would shut her eyes and try to imagine herself dead; or she would argue bitterly with Spenser over small things – over the question, for example, of how many tea-bags should be placed in a tea pot. She took no satisfaction in provoking such arguments, but there was nothing else for her to win.

Spenser never thought about their relationship, which meant that he never thought about her. She would ask him a question and he would acknowledge it with a humming noise; she would say something to him seriously, and he would give her a bewildered gaze as if he had not before noticed her presence. When he left a room, he would often turn the light off although she was still sitting in it.

But, in acknowledged obeisance to his failure to see or treat her as an adult, she would often adopt a 'little girl' manner. She would become the child whom they had never had, and at such moments he would warm towards her, cuddle her and pat her hair with his hand. She was, one evening, feeling in a particularly plaintive mood. 'I'm hungry, Pops,' she complained to Spenser. 'I want some kind of treat. Yoghourt or bananas.'

'Which will it be, little Lettuce?'

'I don't know, do I?'

Spenser, with a look of infinite parental benevolence,

served her some yoghourt in a dish. She ate it while lying on the bed, staring wide-eyed at the television. 'I'm sleepy, Pops,' she announced at the end of the early evening news. 'I want to have a little nap.' Spenser was about to tiptoe out of the room when the telephone rang. She grabbed at it. 'Hello? Yes, this is me. Hi, how are you? Yes, I'm fine. He's fine. Fine. I'd love to. Oh great. Yes. Fine. Right. Of course. Great. O.K. Good. And, Joan darling, remember not to call me Lettuce for Christ's sake.'

She turned to Spenser with a look of triumph. 'Would you mind terribly if I went out tonight?'

'Where to?'

'I'm going to the ballet. Joan has got some complimentary tickets.'

'That old bag.'

'If she has tickets, she is not a bag.' Joan was Laetitia's oldest friend, but she made only a perfunctory effort to defend her.

In fact, Spenser did not in the least mind being left alone. He had received a letter from the Film Finance Board which, in a vague and circumlocutory way, intimated that it was interested in Mr Spender's project, that it would like to meet Mr Spender if Mr Spender had the time to meet it, and it remained yours sincerely. He had written to the Board only a week before, outlining his project almost off-handedly – hoping that, if he did not wish for it too fervently it would happen. Now he needed time to work out his approach; he had not of course mentioned the matter to his little love.

As Laetitia dressed, she turned the radio on to a pop station. The music was loud and repetitive – she thought of it as her overture for the night. She was intrigued, also, by the third member of this surprise party – a young man who, Joan had just confided to Laetitia, was fabulous. Just fabulous, darling. And absolutely devoted to yours truly. This was why Laetitia was now putting on her expensive Harvey Nichols dress, and had warned Joan not to call her Lettuce.

Fabulous was not quite the word she would have used, she thought, when the three of them met outside Covent Garden tube station. But she supposed that it would do.

46

'Lettuce, I mean Laetitia darling, how are you, my poppet?' Joan embraced her so warmly that there was clearly some other impulse struggling within her to be freed. 'I want you to meet Andrew Christopher, darling. Isn't it a wonderful name? He's been dying to meet you for ages, haven't you, poppet?' Andrew Christopher was tall, with a beard that seemed to reveal rather than conceal his lips, and eyes that gleamed as if a match had been struck behind them. 'It's nice to meet you at last, Laetitia.' He practically stared at her, she thought, as if she were a statue in a museum or something. Laetitia smiled at the stare. The stare smiled back. 'It really is a treat meeting you. Joan is so terribly secretive about all her friends.'

'Well, poppets, that's enough of the introductions. Shall we make a move?'

Throughout the ballet, a contemporary version of *Jeux d'Enfants*, Laetitia felt the pressure of Andrew's leg against hers. It was by no means certain that he was actually pushing against her; he might have left his leg there by accident. But, still, it was noticeably and completely there. She felt very warm, as though the heat of his own body were being transmitted to her. The ballet became at once brighter and more difficult to follow; the shapes of the dancers passed in front of her but she could not, for some reason, take them in. She was conscious of his shape beside her, however, like a rock face she was about to climb, like a dream she would experience when she fell asleep.

As soon as the curtain went down, Joan complained that her leg had 'gone to sleep'. As she got up to shake it, she stared objectively at Laetitia as if measuring her for a garment. 'Wasn't that heavenly?' She was speaking to Andrew while still looking at Laetitia.

'It was super. It really was. It's like a Noel Coward play.' This seemed to Laetitia a very wise, and perceptive, thing to say.

'You know', she said, 'I know exactly what you mean. It seems so, well, complete in itself.'

Joan stared at her again. 'Yes, exactly, Laetitia.'

'But then,' Andrew added, 'nothing is ever complete in itself, is it?'

'Oh don't be so silly, Andrew,' Joan had manoeuvred her

stare towards him. 'It's complete as far as the participants are concerned. They are the ones who really know what's going on, don't they, poppet?'

'No, I don't think so, Joan.' He was smiling at Laetitia. 'They're just performers. They could be dancing in a television ad, and it would be all the same to them.' Laetitia smiled back at Andrew, and Joan suddenly became very interested in other members of the audience, peering at them in the way one would watch wild life from the safety of a jeep. The ballet meandered along, and Andrew's leg remained in its previous position throughout.

They had decided – or, rather, social custom decided for them – to have dinner afterwards – 'a quick bite', Joan called it with evident relish. She was, apparently, in good spirits and, while they were waiting for their meal, had two or three large drinks.

'Lettuce – oh sorry, poppet, I meant Laetitia of course – what is Spenser doing these days? Is he still devoted to you?' She looked at Andrew, who was smiling at Laetitia.

'What a lovely name – Lettuce.' He drew it out into a sibilant whisper. 'Does everyone call you that?'

'Only my friends.' She smiled at Joan, who was trying to rub a stain off the top of her dress. 'It makes me sound so lumpish, but I'm used to it now.'

'No, no, it's a lovely name – Lettuce. It sounds like some kind of exotic flower.'

'And so how is Spender, Laetitia?' Joan asked again.

'Oh he's fine. He's always so busy these days I hardly get a chance to see him.'

'And how long is it now, poppet?'

'Since when, Joan?'

'Since you were married, of course.' She smiled at Andrew and brushed a hair off his jacket.

'Oh, five years now, I suppose. But it only sounds like a long time. Honestly, it could just be yesterday.'

'You know, poppet, you really ought to have a child.' Joan patted back her hair. 'You really ought, you know.'

'You're only saying that because you're not married, Joan.' Andrew's tone was almost scolding, as though he had caught her in an act of self-indulgence.

'No, Andrew, Joan is right. I suppose that I just didn't want to burn all my bridges.'

'Bridges of sighs,' Joan said, for no apparent reason.

'And also because Spenser is hardly ever home.' Andrew's leg was now pressed against hers, and she went on talking simply to avert Joan's attention. 'And in any case I don't think it's fair to bring up children in a small flat. Spenser understands – we're like really good friends. Really we are.'

Laetitia smiled at Andrew, and Joan fell upon her food, which had now belatedly arrived, with much cutting and grinding as if it represented some mortal threat. Laetitia drank during dinner and, as she drank, the presence of Andrew grew larger – she could hardly breathe in the space which was left to her. She felt like a moth who had settled upon a lamp – he seemed so close, so warm.

Andrew glowed during dinner; he discussed the ballet, his career as a dancer and then as a model, his friends in the theatre, his hatred of politics and anything to do with racial prejudice. He embraced Joan occasionally; he listened intently to Laetitia; he teased them both for the longevity of their friendship; he asked them about the old days together; he smiled at the waitress when he ordered brandy; he insisted on paying the bill, he would not dream of having them chip in, but all right then if they insisted. Who could stand in the way of women when they had made up their mind about a thing?'

After dinner, they walked to the Strand in search of taxis. 'It's been lovely, Laetitia poppet,' Joan murmured to the sky and to the buildings, 'You and Spenser must come and have dinner with us soon.'

'I've really enjoyed this evening, Lettuce, if I may call you now by the name of that exotic flower.' Andrew gave her shoulder a little squeeze.

'It's a vegetable,' Joan added while flagging down a cab with great urgency.

'So have I, Andrew. And, Joan, you were marvellous to ask me.'

'Well,' Joan suggested as Andrew opened the door for Laetitia, 'we must do it again. Goodbye, Laetitia, and do look after yourself.'

On her way home, Laetitia sat back in the taxi and

pretended to feel bewildered, although she knew in fact that she wasn't. She was experiencing a feeling that she had forgotten existed. She was in charge of her own destiny; she felt that she had jumped off a cliff, and found that she could fly. And Andrew was attracted to her as an independent person, to what she had said. He had seen her as she now saw herself. She closed her eyes, and smiled. When she arrived home, Spenser was already in bed; he turned over in his sleep as she entered the bed, but he did not wake.

eleven

The offices of the Film Finance Board were in a small street off Piccadilly, a newly painted and primped street which still could not quite shake off the sordid and melancholy associations of an alley; the offices themselves were grand, but it was a forced and imposed grandeur. Like a prison or hospital, the stones of the place, the atmosphere of its corridors and its rooms, cast the same shadow over everyone, and that shadow was one of haughty purposelessness.

Spenser Spender, on production of his letter, was, after much staring at it and reading of its contents, taken to a secretary who took him to an assistant who ushered him eventually into the presence of the director of the Board, Sir Frederick Lustlambert, a 'distinguished' man, who, like the building in which he was immured, took care that he looked so and that everybody knew so. His grey hair was curled into neat waves; his suit was of grey silk; his face was grey also, as if it had been conceived and grown in a committee room. His distinction was only marred by the suspicion of a hooked nose which, in profile, made him resemble Punch.

'Mr Spender, how nice of you to come and see us at such very short notice. You are doing us a service, sir.' Sir Frederick's eyes were of the blue that chills, and he held himself erect as though his body were fighting against the ostensible friendliness of his words. 'Well, do please come and sit down. Do please take a chair, my dear fellow.'

Sir Frederick was launched at once, without Spenser Spender having, as it were, to break a bottle against his side, into his theme. '*Little Dorrit* has always been one of my most treasured memories of Dickens, Mr Spender. I haven't read it for many years of course, time is so short, don't you find, for the finer things of life, but the language is so robust, the sentiments so absolutely splendid. I am not what you would

51

call a literary man, Mr Spender, and neither are you I dare say—'

Spenser refused the description with a polite smile.

'—we are film men, film men at heart. But that novel is splendid, simply splendid. And so, when we received your letter, it struck me as a charming idea, quite charming. Exactly, I said to my board, what we are here to assist, in our modest way.'

The profile of Punch turned towards the window, and the nose savoured the aroma of the words before they flew out into the winter air. Spenser was about to be thrilled, thankful, but he was not quite sure what had been said to him.

'Our job, Mr Spender, is not an easy one. We have to work with unions and with government, with—' He struggled to find other groups with whom he had to work, but none occurred to him— 'It is rather dreary to talk of such things but I have to assure my trustees that we are, as it were, financing nothing too political, nothing too risqué. I am forced to wear my government hat. That is why I fell upon *Little Dorrit*, Mr Spender. Here is a subject, I said to my board, upon which we can all agree – a great English classic, a wonderful book, a work of art being filmed in this country, with our superb reservoir of English actors, our pool of English technicians. It could be a triumph, Mr Spender, an absolute triumph. I was most impressed by your prison documentary – you took what I call the broad view, not trying to score narrow political points. The broad view. And so, I said to my board, this is just the man for this project' – he blew his nose with a handkerchief as large as a sail – 'this English epic.' The idea, it seemed, had always been Sir Frederick's, and he had sprung it upon Spenser as a delightful surprise. Sir Frederick sat back and smiled, distinction satisfied, distinction reinforced.

'Does this mean,' Spenser asked, 'that you will finance my project?'

'We will be delighted to do so. I am just reaching that very point. I am a film man, Mr Spender – both of us are film men, are we not?' Spenser nodded politely again. 'And we will pay each other the compliment of being frank with each other. Government bodies are strange beasts, I can't pretend to you otherwise and I wouldn't want to. It is difficult for men like ourselves, but sometimes we must play up and play the game. At times like this I have to wear my civil service hat and say to you, a year will have to be enough, Mr Spender. And there is one other condition.'

The wearing of the invisible hat had somehow affected Sir Frederick's throat, and the voice had become low and confidential.

'I have to think of budgets, you know. And I am afraid that the unions, being what they are – a frightful bore, but I have to think of them, I have to bring them round – well, in short, we have been asked to use the British Theatre Company on this one. Now I know, dear chap, there are certain objections in principle to this. I myself made them forcibly. But we must see round the subject. We must take, as you do, the broad view. Naturally a director should have full freedom in his choice of performers – I put this point to my board. I don't mince my words where my directors are concerned. I wear my chairman's hat. I preside. But, not to put too fine a point on it, they insisted. Our friends on the theatre side are having the devil of a time convincing the government that the British Theatre has, as it were, any purpose, any raison d'être—' the nose sniffed at the phrase – 'and to use them in this film would be a great blessing. One might almost say a relief. It would mean, shall we say, value for money.' The chill blue eyes suddenly enlarged, and Spenser looked momentarily away. 'We can discuss matters of editing and production at a later stage. I know – I am a film man, myself – that you will want to get involved in that. You should be – you are – an artist to the fingertips. I am merely your humble servant.'

Sir Frederick paused, to demonstrate his new servile status. The distinction was still there but he had, as it were, allowed it to rest. Spenser Spender stared at him and could think of nothing to say. A stranger had handed to him a large and elaborate parcel: it would be uncivil of him to return it, but he was too nervous to open it. It was unnerving, also, to discover that his project, which he had hugged so closely to himself that it had in a sense become part of him, had already been the subject of meetings, conversations, arguments and Sir Frederick putting on his various hats. It made him uneasy.

'May I think about what you have said, Sir Frederick, and talk to you later?'

'Of course, my dear fellow, take all the time you need. I am sure myself it is going to be a magnificent project. Superb cinema, utterly superb. By the way, it would be an enormous help if you could let me know by the end of the week – I have this frightful budgetary meeting, and I would be so grateful to have your last word on it by then.'

A bottle of sherry was now brought out, and Sir Frederick put on his relaxed hat. They were men of the world, both of them, wasn't that so? And oh, by the way, before he forgot, his friends on the literary panel had mentioned a very promising young novelist who was writing about Dickens. Chap called Rowan Phillips – ring any bells? No, Spenser's bells had not rung. Well, he might be just the man to do the script for them. That was entirely up to Spenser, of course, but do give him a tinkle – soothe the feelings of the literary mob down the road.

Spenser Spender left the Film Finance Board in a state of profound depression. He had expected his initial enthusiasm to lose some of its first glow but not, with the first taste of success and realisation, to disappear so completely. He had gone in as an inventor, as a free agent, and had come out as a servant – or, rather, as an employee. *Little Dorrit* now encompassed the Board, the British Theatre, let alone Sir Frederick and his hats; it had become anonymous and more threatening. But he was not about to turn down Sir Frederick's offer; it would be like turning down *Little Dorrit* itself. He would have to fight hard to retain the original spirit he had created, but he knew also that this transition was an inevitable one. *Little Dorrit* was no longer his fantasy.

It was, now, a reality. The men trudged around the yard unwillingly, and few of them spoke. When they did so, they sounded curiously muted as if 'exercise' restrained or enervated them. 'You know the same ground rules apply as before, Mr Spender, in by six o'clock and out by six o'clock.'

They were watching the prisoners from a doorway, protected from the cold wind: watching them 'in play-time', as the governor put it, seemed to be a kind of ceremony for outside visitors. It proved, for one thing, how safe and well-regulated the prison was. The prisoners themselves hardly noticed, or cared, that they were being watched.

Suddenly there was a diversion in the yard when one of the prisoners – a dwarf, Spenser thought, or something like it – started singing in a curiously low voice, 'The bells are ringing, for me and my girl.' There was something odd about the sound of it, as though the wrong tune were being used. As he sang, the little prisoner moved out of line and kicked against the wall of the yard. The other inmates paid no attention to his action, but an officer went up to him and guided him back into line.

'Who was that?' Spenser had turned to the governor, who appeared not to have noticed anything at all.

'You know the rules, Mr Spender. No names, no pack-drill. Just hang on a moment, though.' He whispered to the officer next to him, who whispered something back. 'His name is Arthur Feather, Mr Spender. But I'm sure he won't be suitable for your film.'

'What's the matter with him?'

'There's something the matter with all of this lot, isn't there?' He nodded his head, as if in greeting, towards the prisoners in the yard; they were on 'Rule 43', segregated from the rest of the prison population because of the nature of their crime or their behaviour – sex offenders, informers, the lowest class in the prison.

'I'll tell you the matter with Feather, though: he shouldn't be here at all. He should be in a mental hospital. That's the matter with him.' Little Arthur smiled and winked at the governor.

It had been agreed that Spenser could use the abandoned wing of the prison in order to film those sequences which took place inside the Marshalsea debtors' prison, where Little Dorrit had been born. Spenser had insisted upon realism. Sir Frederick Lustlambert, wearing his bureaucratic hat, had written to the Home Office; the Home Office, having pondered upon the hat, wrote to the governor of the prison. The wing had not been in use for fifteen years and the governor, thinking that for once some good publicity might result from the arrangement, agreed.

Spenser knew the prison from his last film: the stale air was like the exhalation of failure. He knew the metal landings and the thick green metal doors upon each cell; he knew the thud of doors being slammed shut in the distance; he knew the corridors in which, at each turning, there would be bars. As always, he found it difficult to look at the prisoners as he passed them; in a sense they claimed invisibility, and to look at them was to take away the one thing – their privacy – which they might hope to retain. He felt, as always, that he had become 'them', the great establishment outside. As always, he wanted to announce that he was really 'us'.

He had wanted to know if the cells still in use were the same as those along the abandoned wing. The officer escorting him smiled faintly: 'The pattern doesn't vary, sir, year by year. Twelve by six it is and always will be – here, take a look at this one just to refresh your memory.' He opened a spy hole in one of the cells, and unwillingly Spenser put his eye to it. A young man lay on his bunk, face down, but when he heard the scraping against the door he raised his head wearily to look at the offending eye. Their eyes met, for one prolonged moment, and Spenser jerked his head away from the cell door in horror. It was Pally in there. He had seen him only a few weeks before outside the Soho pub, a kind of wraith in the pouring rain. He couldn't be here: he was too innocent, too ungainly, too much apart from the world. And then Spenser remembered what the governor of this place had said of the dwarf: he had not belonged here, either.

Perhaps he should say something, admit he knew him, tell the officer he went to school with him – anything at all, so that they might think of him as a person rather than an inmate. Instead, he asked, 'What is that young man here for, officer?'

'Assault, GBH. Same old thing, sir, it never varies, does it?'

Spenser Spender said nothing for a while, and then asked if he might see the abandoned wing, his film set.

56

Pally had been in a dazed slumber before hearing the noises at the door, but now he sat on the edge of his bunk and stared at the floor, as if it were a book which might reveal to him his fate. My name is Pally – he spoke out loud and banged his heels against the floor as he did so – and where I go I am trouble. I close me eyes and I am some place else. I know who brings me there and I can't help it. I seen him three times now. First time he looks through me as if I am daft or some such thing. Second time he calls me, through the thunder, but he is trouble and I hop it. Now I seen him in this place and he is after me. I done nothing. I close my eyes and I am here. I ain't daft as he said. I see what I see and I hear what I hear. That one means trouble.

It was dark by the time Spenser Spender left the prison. The great door closed behind him and the faint noises of institutional life – the shouts and calls, the sound of feet echoing down corridors – faded; but there still lingered with him that depression which affects the spirits of all those who enter a prison. A kind of hopelessness hovers in the air as pervasively as the smell of prison itself, that sense of futility which arises from an oppressive environment which cannot now be altered or destroyed. Such places will always exist – once the Marshalsea, now here. Only a small time – an historical moment – separated the two; and they represented the same appalling waste of human life. Nothing had really changed in a society which had such places as its monuments.

Such were Spenser Spender's confused thoughts as he walked out into the thoroughfare. Perhaps they were coloured by the fact that Laetitia had gone away. Without her presence, Spenser became aware again of that thing, that dark thing, which was always waiting to make itself felt – the sense of the emptiness of his own life. And then he remembered what Lettuce had said to him, just before she left for the holiday with her mother. They had been walking by the river, talking about the past in the rueful tones of people who ought to have known better at the time. Lettuce had turned to Spenser: 'And yet,' she said, 'the saddest people are capable of the greatest happiness.' What had she meant by that?

Above him the sky was clear, and he could see the constellations in perfect order: Orion, Ursa Major, and there also the Pleiades, shining down upon him as he walked towards home.

twelve

After the seance in Ealing, Audrey had been having more of her funny turns. At the seance itself, she had woken out of her trance and stared brightly around the room as if seeing it for the first time. And then quite suddenly she had clapped her hand over the mouth, and got up from the table, knocking her chair over as she did so. At this point her friend, Margery, had asked for a taxi to be called and blow the expense. All the way home, Audrey had said the most peculiar things, like 'Bless you, my love, my dearest love' – addressed apparently to Margery – and 'Poor, poor creature', addressed apparently to herself.

The next morning, at work, everything seemed back to normal. Margery had decided not to mention the incident to the other girls: least said soonest mended was her motto, which came in handy at a telephone exchange. And she didn't want Audrey made a spectacle of.

'Good morning, Marge,' Audrey said brightly as she clocked in. 'And how are we today?'

'Good morning, Aud. Lovely morning, isn't it?'

'That's good, then.' Audrey was looking just over the top of Margery's head as she spoke.

The other girls in the exchange were gathering themselves together for the day, arranging the rows of switches on their boards with evident distaste, sipping tea from plastic cups and clearing their throats, taking one last look in their pocket mirrors as small lights flashed and beamed around them. Then, by general consent, they all began work at once, flicking levers, tapping out telephone codes on the consoles, answering inaudible enquiries, speaking into the receivers with an air of bright disinterest. But the rhythm of their work set its own pace, which was a slow one. The brightness vanished, leaving only the disinterest behind, and sporadic

59

but lengthy conversations began between the operators.

'Did you see the way he looked at Christine in the canteen? He needs his head examining he does. The number you want, madam, is 106. Sex, sex, sex, that's all he thinks about. Anyway, so Christine was meant to do Wednesday's night shift. And what kind of trouble are you having, sir? And so she turned round to him and said. I'm sorry that number has been disconnected. Thank you. She said, ta very much but I'm not interested. You should have seen his face. Yes, can I help you?' All around them the silent machines winked and flashed, emitting an occasional and unpredictable buzz. From time to time, the girls would glance at each other as they talked.

'You're a bit quiet today, Aud,' the girl to Audrey's left said, 'anything the matter?'

'No, I'm fine, Doreen, really I am. That number is ex-directory, sir. I'm sorry. I can't do any more.'

'That's good then. Oooh, I almost forgot, did you two go to that whatdyoumecallit, that seance, last night?'

'We did go in the end,' Margery explained. She suddenly became very interested in the problem of a crossed line which had been brought to her attention.

'Did you see anything, then?'

'No not really, Doreen. I'm afraid I can't help you, madam. I suggest you dial again.'

Doreen was not to be put off. 'I know there's something to it nowadays, but I don't see the sense in it myself – all that mucking around with the dead and buried. 192 for enquiries outside London. And thank you. It gives me the heeby-jeebies just thinking about it.' She gave a quick glance at Audrey, who had remained silent and apparently preoccupied with her work. She decided to try a new subject.

'Did you see the way the new supervisor looked at you this morning, Aud? Stripping you with his eyes that's what he was doing. Rather you than me really.'

'Something did happen last night, Doreen, if you really want to know.' Audrey's voice was shaky. Several other girls, although engaged in conversation with various parties at the other end of the line, looked sideways at her.

'Go on then. Don't keep us in suspense.'

'I was taken over by someone.'

Doreen giggled. 'Give over. And pull the other one it's got bells on.' She lit up a cigarette, and ignored the light which was flashing in front of her.

'Marge will tell you. She saw it too.'

Margery stared straight ahead of her, and did not look at the other girls. 'I think it was just the novelty of it, Aud,' she said, 'It could happen to anyone really.'

'Go on, Marge, you might as well tell them.'

By lunch-time, the whole floor knew that something odd had happened to Audrey Skelton; that she had moaned and whispered at the back of a taxi; that Margery had practically fainted on the spot. Audrey's reputation for being too clever by half was now modified to one of her being not quite right in the head.

It was after this that things started to go wrong. Some days, Audrey would just stare at her board for minutes at a time; she would try and engage certain callers in conversation and she would give others deliberately false information. She had bought a shawl, second-hand, and would work with it wrapped around her. The girls in the canteen said that they felt more sorry for Tim, really, than anything else.

Tim was, indeed, bewildered by Audrey's behaviour. She had bought him a copy of *Little Dorrit*, and insisted that he read it. He had started reading the introduction, by an academic, thinking it was the novel itself, and as a result abandoned the book as useless. Audrey, however, would still read out significant passages to him. She would adopt various voices and make strange noises, while she did so; and, when she acted Little Dorrit herself, her voice would take on a curious pleading and whispering quality which was, to Tim, quite disagreeable. It didn't seem right, or natural.

Under the stress of these events, he went swimming more and more frequently. But, as he swam relentlessly lap after lap in the local baths, the sounds and shouts of the pool seemed to him more like echoes of a mad house, a vast chamber of disorder. The murder of the girl by the now notorious Little Arthur had upset him almost as much as Audrey's behaviour. He could remember Little Arthur and Fun City from the time of his childhood, and now that world had been snatched from him. His life had ceased to be the humdrum but comforting affair which it had always seemed. Audrey herself served as an image of what was happening: he thought he knew her better than anybody, but now he could no longer be sure of her. He began to dread the thought of seeing her. What made it worse was that there was no one with whom he could discuss such things. Anyway, he thought, I don't have the words for it. It's just this funny feeling.

He was sitting at home with his parents, watching football on television, when the telephone rang. Calls in the evening were rare, and often meant trouble of some kind. His mother, being the extrovert in the family, answered it.

'It's for you, our Tim.'

'Is it Audrey?'

'No, some foreigner. I didn't catch his name.'

He went uneasily towards the phone, holding it to his ear as if it were a revolver.

'Hello? Is that Timothy Coleman?'

'Yeah, this is me.'

'Oh hi, Timothy. This is Rowan Phillips – do you remember we met last month?'

'Oh yeah, Mr Phillips. That's right. We met.'

'Well, I guess I was just wondering if we could make that trip some time. Round old London and all.' Rowan, out of nervousness, was slightly overdoing the accent.

'Could you just hang on a minute? The kettle's boiling.'

Tim sat on the stairs, and pondered. Audrey had said that she wanted to meet Rowan Phillips again, but her moods were unpredictable. He didn't want Mr Phillips to be embarrassed by her, as so many of his friends now were. He rubbed his face. But he was a writer, wasn't he, and used to dealing with other people's problems? He might give him some good advice. He might, what do you say, psychoanalyse Audrey. He picked up the phone again.

'Sorry about that, Mr Phillips. I dropped the tea-pot.'

'That's fine, Tim. Don't worry about a thing.'

'Sure. Right. Well, that's a good idea. We'll look around some of London. Great.'

'Shall I meet you some place, Tim?'

'Well, Audrey's got a bit of a head cold, so why don't we meet by the Marshalsea tube? – you know, where all the tramps are.'

'Okay. Now when will that be, Tim?'

'Sunday around dinner time suit you?'

'Dinner?' Rowan thought it might be too dark by then to see very much of anything.

'Yeah, about oneish. Let's say 1.00.'

'That will be just fine, Tim. I'll look forward to it.'

'Oh, right. That's all right then.'

The 'phones were replaced, although Rowan waited for Tim to put his down first: he wanted to hear him breathing. Such sweet breath. Tim went back to the television. Now at last there was hope – someone clever he could talk to about Audrey. Rowan Phillips lay back on the bed, his stomach churning. Tim hadn't said anything about Audrey joining them; perhaps he would come alone. Perhaps they could spend the afternoon together. Perhaps Tim was secretly attracted to him. He undid his trousers and, thinking of Tim with his hair sleeked back and damp and walking towards him, he decided to masturbate. He wanted the best of both worlds, but one would do for the moment.

thirteen

Laetitia hadn't gone on holiday with her mother, as she had told Spenser. She had gone instead to Shepherd's Bush, to the flat of Andrew Christopher. Their first meeting in Covent Garden had instigated a delicately phrased telephone call from Andrew, during which, in an offhand way, lunch was suggested. It was intimated that Joan might have business elsewhere that day, and Andrew longed to talk more with Laetitia about life. Her judgments had seemed so right, so marvellous. Over lunch, Andrew had gazed at her lovingly – although to Laetitia the gaze still faintly resembled a stare. He had taken her hand: may he call her Lettuce? She had withdrawn her hand, but had met his gaze with her own. He could not hide what he felt, he was not that kind of person: he wanted to sleep with her that minute, or at least that afternoon. She asked him about Joan; Joan, it turned out, was just a friend really. Nothing serious. Andrew's tone was gentle and sympathetic – Joan was a sweet thing, really. He asked her about Spenser, and she pretended to become slightly fretful and impatient. He was work, work, work. All work and no play, Andrew suggested in his most playful manner.

It was only when she woke up next to Andrew, on that first morning in Shepherd's Bush, that Laetitia wondered if she had betrayed Spenser in some way. But that was all mental, just in the head: she had read something in the *Guardian* about it only the other day. She looked down at her own body, uncovered now as Andrew turned in his sleep and wrapped the sheets about him. She looked at herself as impersonally as she could, and was surprised to find how good, how slender, she seemed. She wanted to turn on the radio, and listen to a song.

But Andrew, in the last stages of sleep, had an erection and in a half-dream he pulled Laetitia towards him. She took care to avert her face and breathe across him, just in case her breath were not fresh. Automatically, he had done the same. They had sex while looking over each other's shoulders. Afterwards, they lay side by side and stared at the ceiling. Laetitia was too self-conscious to look Andrew in the face, in case he discovered some blemish upon her own. But Andrew was thinking of other things.

'What's Spenser like in bed?'

'How do you mean, Andrew?'

'You know, Lettuce. Is he a good lover?'

'He isn't bad, I suppose. He's very careful with me.' Andrew was tapping his foot on the end of the bed; he was obviously waiting for something else. 'He's not as good as you, though.'

'It's just practice, my darling.' He smiled at her, and went into the bathroom to brush his teeth. He shouted at her through the sound of taps running. 'Today, Lettuce, I want us to have fun. I want to show you absolutely everything: my friends, my places, just everything. Let's have coffee or something, and then lunch together at Fortnum's. Do you know Marisa Cambridge? She is one wonderful singer, and I said we'd meet her at the Lagoon tonight. I just can't wait for you to meet her. She happens to be one of my dearest and oldest friends.'

The last thing Laetitia wanted was to wander all over London on Andrew's arm, especially since she was supposed to be in Somerset with her mother. She had to remind herself that she was a mature adult – her body proved it, and their sex together reinforced it. Her mind would simply have to catch up with that evident fact. She would brave the city.

Marisa Cambridge was as effusive with Andrew as Andrew was with her: it was as if they were in an effusiveness competition. But after the hugs and the kisses and the compliments, it was clear that they had very little left to say. They proclaimed their undying love for each other, and then waited for Laetitia to change the subject. She started talking, and then they decided it was time to order more drinks. They would greet each friend who arrived with hugs and expressions of amazement, that they couldn't believe their luck.

'Come and join our table,' Andrew or Marisa would say. 'Do you know Laetitia Spender? You know. Her husband, the film director.' Laetitia hoped to God that they didn't. She smoked and smiled wildly at every remark. The table was by now talking about its previous night, about whom it saw and what it thought. It had been, it seemed, generally unimpressed.

'Did you see Dustin last night,' the table asked Laetitia. 'Honestly, he looked *so* flaky. He said he hated making that film with Carlotta.'

'No, I didn't,' Laetitia said, 'I missed him.'

'He was with that frightful little deb, you know.'

'I think so.'

Andrew was by now becoming more expansive than usual, signalling to people across the night-club, making strange hand signals to the waiters, getting up with a loud cry of joy and hugging almost everyone who passed the table. The table itself made no reaction to these events – in fact, it seemed to have very few reactions of any kind. 'Spenser Spender,' Andrew told it, with Laetitia smiling wanly beside him, 'is enormously talented. He's just got this American money for his new film.' Laetitia wondered how Andrew knew this, but she accepted it as an evident fact and one more example of the way Spenser neglected to tell her anything of importance.

'Marisa,' Andrew went on, 'you were so *good* last night. You are the most incredibly talented lady.' A young man with a camera wandered past. 'Oh, no press! No press!' Andrew put his hands up to his face in mock horror. The table smiled indulgently, as if it had indeed been in imminent danger of being photographed.

'Wasn't Sara Hammond-Watson a nightmare last night?' Andrew was engrossing the table. 'She's so vulgar about all her money – she thinks she's so classy. God, I hate that lady.' Laetitia was impressed by the names of these people whom she had only previously come across in the gossip columns; Andrew obviously knew them all. She drew in her cigarette, and let the smoke out slowly. She smiled at Andrew. He took her face in his hands: 'You know, Lettuce, you are one most sophisticated lady.'

The table smiled at them and drank its relatively inexpensive champagne.

fourteen

Rowan Phillips arrived too early at Marshalsea; he didn't want to miss Tim and, in his eagerness, he had come fifteen minutes too soon. The 'down-and-outs' were, as usual, leaning against the walls of the underground station or sitting inside its entrance; a bottle was being handed round, and the young, red-headed tramp was engaged in an animated discussion with two or three others. There seem to be more of them, Rowan thought, although he certainly didn't want to hang around and take a head-count. He walked towards the park which had once been the site of Marshalsea Prison – he savoured the romance in the idea of revisiting an old haunt where Tim and he had been. It was as though they were already lovers; he would pretend for a while that they were. The park was barer and darker, now that late autumn had turned to winter, and there were some odd chalk marks on the path – it looked like the outline of a small bundle, but he couldn't be sure. For some reason his original mood had deserted him; he felt restless and ill at ease. He popped a peppermint in his mouth, and walked towards the station.

Tim was standing there, staring vaguely in the direction of the tramps, as if they were friends he once knew but now could not quite recall. When he saw Rowan walking towards him, he started and rubbed his cheek with his hand. They shook hands awkwardly.

Rowan expressed surprise and disappointment that Audrey was not present. Tim had anticipated this. 'She's not feeling too good, to tell you the truth. But she sends her regards.' He had not, in fact, seen Audrey in more than a week. 'Do you feel like having a pint, like? There's a pub just round the corner.'

This was exactly what Rowan felt like – a place with other

people, with drink, a place to relax. The pub was large and dark, like a waiting room in some forgotten railway station. High in one corner, a television set glowed and shifted. The programme seemed to be some kind of mock-Victorian music-hall, and the tinny sounds of a small orchestra echoed through the vast saloon bar. A young woman, dressed in an approximation to Victorian costume, was singing a sentimental ballad:

> 'Who passes by this road so late?
> Always gay!'

Rowan moved towards a small table in a corner beyond the range of the television, and therefore in more shadow. Tim insisted on buying the drinks: Rowan wanted a gin, but thought better of it. He would have a pint of bitter, cheers and thanks a lot, Tim, although he detested the taste of beer and the vague, unlocatable swelling which it seemed to produce in his body. He sipped at it nervously.

'So how are you then, Tim?'

'Oh I'm all right you know, Rowan. Just the usual, like.'

'How's work?'

'I can't complain, really. Lucky to have a job.'

'Yes, I know. Times are bad.' Rowan in fact knew nothing about such matters; economic conditions began and ended for him in royalty statements.

'It's not so good round here these days, Rowan.'

'Is that so? That's just terrible.'

The music from a juke-box collided with that from the television set, making an awkward counterpoint between the fake Victorian tune and the real contemporary one.

'And how is Audrey getting on?'

'Oh, she's all right. Just a bit under the weather.'

'That's too bad. I was looking forward to seeing her.'

They drank in silence for a while until Rowan, in order to relieve the tension, went up to the bar and ordered the same again, please. When he returned, Tim had twisted around in his chair to face Rowan directly. 'To tell the truth, Rowan, she's not quite herself.'

'Who isn't?'

'Audrey. She went to some seance, like, and she's been acting up a bit odd. Do you know what I mean?'

Rowan didn't, but he nodded. He wanted to gain Tim's confidence. Tim, for his part, wished to gain a writer's insight from Rowan on how to deal with Audrey's moods. Tim did not generally drink very much, and the rapid nervous swallowing of beer was beginning to make him more talkative. He leant forward towards Rowan with a look of intense concentration upon his face: each word was an obstacle which he had to overcome.

'You're a writer, right? Well, anyway, Audrey and I were having this great relationship, right? I'm not mucking you around, it was really great. And now she's gone all peculiar, like. She uses all these strange words and talks about some little porridge or little forehead – I don't know what she's on about. I might as well be a fly on the wall for the attention she pays to me. And then she'll suddenly look at me strange, right, and she'll say I know what you're thinking. You're all talking about me, aren't you. Don't try and lie to me. And honest, I haven't mentioned her to anyone. And then I say to her, to get her on a normal keel like, come on, Aud, let's go to the pictures, or down the pub. And she says, not now. Tomorrow maybe. Not now. I'm thinking.' Tim paused, reflecting upon his own loquacity. 'So what do you think about it all then?' He went to the bar, for more drinks, before Rowan had the chance to answer him.

Rowan could not have been more pleased; here was Tim in distress, and he was asking Rowan for aid and, perhaps, comfort also. Rowan had the ability to understand people without necessarily sympathising with them: he guessed that Audrey was suffering the onset of some form of mild schizophrenia – through sexual frustration, societal repression or whatever. Tim had mentioned Little Dorrit, hadn't he – an odd choice of projection, but interesting. Rowan was also getting a little drunk.

'Tim, I'm going to be honest with you about this. You may not like it, but it's important for you and Audrey to get things straight.'

Tim nodded expectantly. Rowan adopted his clinical

manner, a mild parody of the way in which he conducted his tutorials.

'Do you think, to begin with, that Audrey has homosexual tendencies?'

'How do you mean?'

'Well, do you think that she is attracted to other women?'

'You what?'

'Does she get aroused by women other than herself?'

'Come off it. No. I don't think so.'

'Right. That's alright then. Well, I would imagine, Tim, that somehow Audrey is sexually frustrated. Everyone is to a certain degree, aren't they?'

'I suppose so. I never thought about it, to tell you the truth.'

'I think this business about strange words and using Little Dorrit as a surrogate—'

'I didn't say anything about anyone like that—'

'Oh, didn't you? Well anyway, Tim, the voices and everything suggest to me that she's sexually frustrated. Do you understand what I'm saying? When I saw her, I could tell she was frustrated and depressed.'

Tim looked at Rowan with gratitude: here, at last, was someone who could understand Audrey, and help her. In fact Rowan had noticed nothing whatever about her, except that she talked too much and dressed badly.

'Now, how do people get rid of their frustrations? You go swimming, Tim, right?' Tim nodded: this explanation of the swimming baths was a revelation to him. 'I write books. But other people can't find any outlet, and they want other people to help, right? But they're too proud to ask for help. So they behave in odd ways.' Rowan was pleased with his effort at instant analysis; although he was sure that it did not fit the precise facts of the case, it seemed to have a ring of truth to it.

'What you have to do, Tim, is this. You go and see a doctor, and tell him about Audrey. He will offer to see her, I'm sure. Then you go back to Audrey and tell her that your doctor is very interested in her experience at the seance. Right?' Rowan Phillips knew very little about the National Health Service and, as always, his practical advice was less well constructed than his analytical. But Tim nodded, seeing a plan of action. 'The doctor will soon find out what's wrong and he'll tell her to to see a psychiatrist, probably. He'll probably give her some tranquillisers in the meantime. If she agrees, you'll nip the problem in the bud, right?'

It all sounded so simple, so matter of fact. It was great, Tim thought, when someone brainy comes into it. In his relief, he went to the bar for more drinks.

Now Rowan was thinking even less clearly: the effort of concentrating upon this Audrey woman was beginning to show. But he had made friends with Tim, and now had found the perfect excuse to go on seeing him. Tim, he imagined, was grateful but he didn't want to scare him off by moving too fast. But he hadn't been shocked when he had mentioned lesbianism. Perhaps he accepted such things – Rowan had read somewhere that the London working class were very broad-minded. What had the word been – 'life-enhanced'?

When Tim returned with the drinks, he spilt some on his trousers. Rowan didn't notice; he was moving phrases around in his mind, planning his next move.

'Did it shock you, Tim, when I asked if Audrey had lesbian tendencies?'

'No. She doesn't.'

'No, I know. But the reason I asked is that a lot of people have and don't know about it, and it causes depression. Not just lesbian tendencies, I mean.'

'Oh yeah. I never thought about it really.' Tim rubbed his face, as if trying to remove some blemish.

'You see, Tim, each human being is basically bisexual and it's a mistake to go one way and another.' Rowan meant to say 'or another', but he was drunk now.

'Oh yeah.'

'People have to explore everything they can. We only get one life, right?'

'That's right. One life.'

'You see, Tim, I have to admit that I'm bisexual – probably like Audrey.' It was a lie – Rowan had never kissed a girl, let alone slept with one – but it sounded appropriate.

Tim nodded and shifted in his seat. He thought there was something odd about Rowan. Anyway all writers were a bit

71

queer. He looked round to see if anyone was listening to their conversation.

'Does that shock you, Tim?'

'No. It's your life, right?' Tim tried to look non-shocked, and merely looked nonplussed. 'A man's got to do what a man's got to do.'

'That's right, Tim. That's just it.' Rowan was just sober enough not to press the point: he was going to suggest that they went back to his flat, just for a drink of course. What was that English phrase about taking a horse to drink?

Tim was following his own line of thought.

'I had a friend at school who was queer, like – not like you Rowan, bisensual. He just went after fellers. He used to tell me what he did, and I sort of sat and listened. He was a nice guy though, don't get me wrong, he ended up in the police.'

'That's good, Tim, that's really good.'

The bell rang for closing time, and dispelled Rowan's by now confused sensations. The trip around London was tacitly abandoned, and they walked a little unsteadily out into the cold air of the afternoon. In the daylight, they might easily have become strangers again. But Rowan grasped at the only hold he had over Tim: 'I would do something about Audrey soon, Tim. Ring me next week and tell me how you're getting on. I hate to see the two of you breaking up like this.' He wrote down his telephone number on a piece of paper, and gave it to Tim.

At the entrance to the underground they were about to shake hands when Rowan reached up and kissed Tim awkwardly on the cheek. Tim turned away, and Rowan banged his head on Tim's chin. He smiled, with a combination of resentment and embarrassment, and rushed into the elevator. Tim rubbed his cheek where Rowan had tried to kiss him, and looked around to see if anybody had noticed. The red-headed tramp had seen, but made no reaction: such things were trifling to him. Much the worse for drink, Tim headed for home.

Rowan sensed that he had behaved badly, but was not quite sure how. At such moments he felt that his personality was like some distant planet, and his mind a scanning device, going over it area by area, searching for signs of human life.

When he got back to his flat he started, with a wild effort of will, to make notes on a study of Dickens he was reading, *The Sacred Changeling: Themes of Reversal in 'Little Dorrit'*, when he fell into a deep sleep.

When he woke up, it was already dark; Rowan felt a peculiar sensation of emptiness, as though he had fallen through a hole in time and had become weightless in the process. His head ached. He clutched a pillow to his chest as if trying to ward off some blow. He thought of the previous few hours, and decided to have a bath. Change into something else. Walk out into the night and make amends for the day. He was, he sensed, being unduly optimistic. The night in London promises nothing; it is a bland darkness which gives as little as it promises. In other cities the night is full of movement and possibility; in London, it is like a cloth placed over the cage of a bird.

But Rowan was attempting to escape from himself, and darkness was an appropriate cover. He put on his leather jacket, borrowed from his father some years before and never returned, a white T-shirt and blue jeans. He pulled on, with some difficulty, a pair of Canadian cowboy boots and attached an old and useless bunch of keys to his belt. He rushed out onto the Gray's Inn Road as if he were about to miss an urgent appointment, checked himself and then tried to walk slowly, casually, in order to complement his clothes; in every shop-front he passed, he examined his reflection surreptitiously. But he managed in the process only to look ungainly, twisting and turning as though suffering from some nervous disorder.

The pub he eventually entered was an old one. The wooden benches were chipped and stained, and a large gilt mirror hung askew in a corner. Large velvet drapes covered the windows. Rowan walked self-consciously towards the bar, where a small group of men – all of them similarly dressed in leather and jeans – had already formed, the sound of key-chains jangling as the pints were raised. No one noticed Rowan's arrival, and an elderly man, wearing a leather dog-collar with studs attached, like a malevolent priest, was in the middle of an impassioned monologue. 'Well, if she wants to carry on like a fucking whore, good luck to her. I'm not going to be around to pick up the pieces. She comes swinging in here like Miss Butch, and she goes home with anything. I said to her, you're going to end up with a knife in your fucking back you are.'

The others murmured assent, and their eyes wandered over the pub – one or two now coming to rest on Rowan, who was trying to prop himself up on the bar. His elbow slipped, and he spilt beer over his trousers. 'Someone's got wet already,' the elderly man remarked and smiled at Rowan. His teeth were large, and yellowing. Rowan smiled back, not sure if the remark were hostile or not. He walked over and pretended to read a poster concerning a series of murders in that vicinity; the smell of a fish-and-chip shop next to the pub wafted through each time the door opened.

Two young men stumbled in on roller-skates, to the evident disapproval of the men in leather. The man in the dog-collar stared with a cold lasciviousness at one of them: 'She'll end up on her fucking arse by ten.' The landlady, a lugubrious old party in a blue cardigan, heard the remark: 'And so will you, darling, the way you're going. With all that leather, you won't be able to get up again neither.' The group of men broke apart in hysterical laughter as she wandered away. More remarks were exchanged, and their eyes wandered again.

The pub was now filling up quickly; solitary men came in and sailed up to the bar like tugs looking for a berth. Once a drink was safely in their hand they would wander across the floor, smiling at someone here, pressing accidentally against someone there, generally ending up, aloof, in a convenient area of shadow or half-light, apparently looking at nothing and no one in particular. As Rowan darted self-consciously around, sneaking occasional glances at himself in the gilt mirror, he overheard snatches of conversations. 'I hope she chokes on her come, that one', this from a man with a plaid shirt and glasses who pursed his lips with disapproval. 'Look at that one there, tits like a horse.' Eddies of loud, barking laughter swept across the room. 'Oh God, look what's coming in now.' Occasionally, the eyes of two men would meet and then take fright.

One man smiled nervously at another. The other smiled

back. One went up to the other. The other bought drinks. The leather men, still forming a group, watched the action with disinterested curiosity. In the corner of the bar an old man sat, wearing a red woolly cap and reading the *Standard*; next to him a young man with spiky hair, wearing an old and now tattered raincoat. He was staring at everyone and smiling, rubbing his eyes and looking down at his feet if anyone happened to smile back.

Rowan felt unwanted; deliberately he walked past the two men who had just met, to hear what they were saying. They were discussing football. One man was tracing his finger over the back of the other's hand. Rowan knew that the secret of success in such places as this was to think you were attractive, and then behave as such. He threw out his shoulders, raised his head and, with a slight smile, walked over to the bar again. A group of four young men, in denim overalls, was standing close to him. 'I fancy him over there,' one denim was saying, 'He's got ever such nice eyes.' 'Go up to him then, you daft cow,' another denim nudged him reproachfully, 'Tell him you want a light for my cigarette.' Rowan assumed that it was he who was being discussed; he tried to widen his eyes slightly, since he had read that this increased one's attractiveness. He smiled at the boy, who seemed to respond by smiling broadly back; Rowan tried shyly to meet his eyes, and then noticed that the boy was actually looking past him. Rowan half-turned and saw a young man with blond hair further down the bar – lounging with the self-confidence of someone who is used to being looked at. Rowan was angry now: he was being looked through. Immediately, he hated the place and everyone in it. And then he thought of Tim – if he came in here, they would all want him. That blond prick wouldn't stand a chance.

Comforted somewhat, he moved away from the bar, walking haughtily past the young man with the blond hair, and stood against the wall in such a position that what he imagined to be his 'best' profile could be seen. Once again, he pretended to read the murder poster on the wall. Someone else was standing in front of him; from the back, Rowan thought, he looked large and warm. He could only speculate about the front. He watched him surreptitiously, in case the

75

face came into sight. The man turned suddenly towards Rowan: 'Would you watch my drink a second, mate, while I go to the loo?' Such frankness, Rowan thought. He nodded. The man looked good. He looked comfortable. He would certainly do for the night. When the man returned, Rowan smiled. It was important to keep up the momentum.

'Have you been here before?' Rowan kept the smile upon his face, as if it had been plastered upon it.

'Quite a few times.'

'Is it always this crowded?'

'Yeah. You can't move on a Saturday night.'

The ritual exchanges over, Rowan searched for something else to say – some new avenue towards the man's attention.

'So this is your local, is it?' Rowan leaned towards him, hoping that his breath did not smell excessively of drink, or anything else.

'You could say that. Where are you from, then?'

'Cambridge.'

'What's the gay scene like there then?'

'Oh pretty dead, you know. There's only one gay bar.'

The man whistled between his teeth; he had turned fully round to face Rowan now. 'Is that a fact then?'

'What do you do?' Rowan asked. He knew that he was getting the order of questions confused, but he plunged on regardless.

'What, in bed?'

'No. I mean for a living.'

'I'm a house-painter. What do you do then?'

'I'm a teacher.'

'Is that right?'

'Yes. It is.'

Rowan was becoming bored with the conversation, and pressed his leg against the man, who did not move away. He smiled instead. The compact was almost made; the gestures needed now were few and predictable, like a ritual of which the meaning had been forgotten. Five minutes later, they left the bar together. The leather men watched them go, incurious.

The man's flat was small, but it was cluttered with ornaments

76

and mementoes: a statuette of a man on a horse, a vase filled with paper flowers, a pair of castanets nailed to the wall, a poster of Bette Midler. A small dog sniffed around Rowan's trousers as he stood self-consciously in the middle of the room. The man watched him for a moment. They kissed, went into a tiny bedroom, and took off their clothes. They both wanted to be the active partner and, by mutual but unspoken consent, decided instead to masturbate each other. The small dog lay at the end of the bed and watched. When they had both come, the man groped under the bed for a box of Kleenex tissues. He lit a cigarette, as Rowan began to dress.

'Well,' Rowan addressed the air, 'I have to be going now.'

'I guess so then.'

'Okay. Well, I'll see you around.'

'Yeah. I'll be seeing you then.'

The man showed Rowan to the door and then, relieved, went back into his little flat, fed his small dog and switched on the portable television. Rowan walked into the street and hailed a taxi. It was raining now, and small cold drops ran through the leather jacket and on to his skin. He hardly felt them. He stared out at the dark and empty streets of London. At least he would get to bed early for once.

fifteen

Spenser Spender still remembered the name Penstone. Spenser combined selfishness with method, so that he kept anything that might be useful to him: even if, in this case, it was only a name scribbled upon a cigarette packet. Penstone was a lecturer, or somethinng like that. Hadn't he made a special study of *Little Dorrit*? There were five Penstones in the telephone directory and he would have to 'phone each one in turn, his natural lack of interest in other people (which was often mistaken for shyness) over-ruled now by the demands of the film. He found Penstone after ringing a chiropractor and what sounded like a sports stadium.

Yes, Penstone remembered their conversation in the restaurant. He sounded guarded – whether out of suspicion or embarrassment, it was impossible for Spenser to tell. They agreed to meet; or rather Spenser – to make the friendly gesture, since he was after all seeking Penstone's advice – asked if he could come and see him.

Job Penstone lived in Archway, down one of those long, tree-lined streets which transform North London into a kind of maze; depending on which particular corner you turn, you are confronted either by unredeemed squalor or by the vague dilapidation of large and perhaps once grand houses. The air is chillier here, the trees darker, the streets gloomier, covered by a further encrustation of grime and urban decay.

Penstone's door was opened for Spenser by a young man wearing a red cloth band around his forehead which pushed up a mass of thin, but still curly, hair.

'Does Mr Penstone live here?'

'Right on, man. Come right in.'

The hallway was dark, the only brightness coming from a number of crudely designed and printed posters which had been fixed haphazardly to the walls: Unite Against Tory

Cuts. Solidarity Meeting. Socialist Youth League in Revolt. Women Against Racism.

Job Penstone came down the stairs, his tweed jacket and ancient corduroy trousers oddly out of place with the patina of modern life which surrounded him. 'Mr Spenser? Do come on up please.' The guardedness was still there, but there was also a faintly apologetic note to his voice – as if the conversation might in some subtle sense be impaired by the presence of so young a sensibility on the posters downstairs. They walked up a steep staircase to the second floor, into a room which Penstone called his 'den'.

'I'm sorry about the mess.' He pointed towards a chair, as if the chair was responsible for it. 'Since my wife left me, I've become more and more untidy. She'd be most upset if she knew.' He said this with a curious satisfaction, like a small boy defiant.

'Was that your son downstairs, actually? The one who answered the door?'

'Oh no, not at all. That was one of my students. There are four of them living – the housing shortage being what it is, Mr Spenser, one had to do one's bit for democratic socialism, open up a few rooms and so forth.' His face, Spenser could see now, was heavily lined, sunk in slightly, as if with the effort of thought, or simply with the pressures of the reality which he had inflicted upon himself.

'And so you're working on a film, Mr Spenser. I wish you luck. I tried my hand with one at the polytechnic, but the enthusiasm of the staff was not, shall we say, forthcoming.'

'Well, I have had some experience of films, actually. It's really all I know about.' Spenser felt like the ambassador of some primitive republic, called in to justify the habits of his race. 'All the same,' he added apologetically, '*Little Dorrit* is a new departure for me. I don't want to ruin the book, or anything like that.'

Job Penstone lit his pipe and, as he did so, his eyes glazed over. It was as if he could not light his pipe and think at the same time. 'Ah yes, *Little Dorrit*. It's a profound work, Mr Spenser—'

'Please just call me Spenser.' He was getting tired of being called by the wrong name.

'It's a profound work, Mr Spenser, a profound descriptive work. I am not at all convinced that it will take easily to film.'

Let me worry about that, was Spenser's unspoken reaction. But he attempted instead to look thoughtful – 'Which was really why I wanted your advice, Job. I want to get it right.'

'You know, Mr Spenser, there is a paradox, an ambiguity, here. It would seem to me that, in essence as it were, *Little Dorrit* is a powerful exposé of social conditions – of social conditioning, one might say. An indictment, one might add, of industrial capitalism. And yet here we are planning a film version – which is, you might say, an expression of Western capitalism.'

Spenser had not realised that they were planning anything at all, but Job Penstone clearly enjoyed the sensation – even vicariously – of organisation, meetings, involvement.

The door was suddenly opened. 'Do you want a cup of char, Job?' It was the young man again. 'And how about the squire here?' He gave a quizzical look at Spenser, who smiled uneasily back. 'That would be very nice, Peter. Thank you indeed. For two? For two, yes.'

'I understand what you're saying, Job.' Spenser tried to gain some initiative in the conversation. 'But the whole direction of the film, actually, will be to make a contemporary point. About socialism, as you said.' Penstone had not said that, but Spenser was sure that he would think he had. 'About the poverty, and all that sort of thing. Did you see my television film on prisons, actually?'

'No. I don't believe I did. I wish I had. It is a pity I didn't. It would have given more, er, meat to our discussion. But I see the point you're trying to make. I see the point.' Like many other moderately clever men, Job Penstone was always ready to 'see the point' which others were 'trying' to make, even if he had not actually grasped it. 'I would say this to you, then, Mr Spenser, by all means go ahead with your film—' as if Spenser were now asking permission to do so— 'but remember that *Little Dorrit* is a subversive text. It is significantly anti-capitalist, anti-industrial, anti-authoritarian. But at the same time, Mr Spenser, remember that you and indeed I are working in a culture which is all these things: capitalist,

80

industrialist, and authoritarian. There is a paradox here and, as I may have said, an ambiguity.'

Spenser Spender had understood this several minutes before, but he nodded sagaciously and humbly as the knowledge was once again imparted to him.

'So how would you suggest that I handle locations, characters, all that sort of thing?'

The young man came in with two mugs of tea; as he handed one to Spenser, he made a subservient bow, and then winked. Job Penstone did not appear to notice this or, if he did, was too familiar with such behaviour to remark upon it. 'As to location, Mr Spenser, you have no problem there. There is as much poverty or, as we prefer to call it, social deprivation, in London now as there was in the nineteenth century. Will you stay to dinner, by the way? It is a modest affair, but our own.' Job Penstone was obviously warming to his theme, and would take some time to cool down. Spenser hardly had time to agree.

'There is as much social deprivation then as now. Only its outward form has changed. Dickens was attacking the use of brute power by the ruling classes to preserve its own interests; at the same time, Mr Spenser, he was describing the struggle of the working classes to preserve themselves – their native culture, their powers of vernacular expression, all the rich ambience of working-class life. Do you get my point, Mr Spenser?' Spenser thought so.

'Good. Well, the book is essentially about that conflict. Nowadays the power in our society is exercised – shall we say, more discreetly? They don't imprison Little Dorrit for debt; they force her into petty crime and then institutionalise her in a borstal. We are not all ruined by the financial machinations of one individual. We – the working class, that is – are ruined by the internationalist capitalist system of repression. And there,' he said triumphantly, 'there is your theme!'

Job Penstone sipped at his tea and then, with a dirty handkerchief, wiped the sweat from his forehead. Spenser Spender was prepared to believe that there was a certain justice to Penstone's argument, if indeed it was an argument, but it seemed to bear very little relation to the book he was about to film. An organised system of repression might exist.

81

But it would be extremely difficult to photograph. For no apparent reason, he recalled the image of Pally in his cell.

'And what about the notion of imprisonment, Job? How could that be related to the film?'

'Well, there you have the perfect example.' Penstone had brought out his handkerchief again – his thoughts were making him sweat. 'What else can you do with the legitimate grievances of the working class except repress them? What do you do with the representatives of the working class except lock them up? It is happening now in England. Even in the socialist countries it is happening. Dickens was a great social prophet, Mr Spenser. Put that in your film, and see how the establishment reacts to it.'

Someone knocked loudly on the door and intoned, in the manner, if not the vocabulary, of a Thirties butler, 'Grub is up, squire.'

Job and his guest went down to the basement of the house, into a large kitchen. Four young people sat at a wooden table, silent, as if in homage to the food which was heaped in three large bowls. Spenser could not make out what, in fact, the food consisted of. 'This is Spender, everyone,' Job Penstone announced unceremoniously. The four looked at him without interest, as though one human being or so extra in the world could make no conceivable difference. The food was spooned out; Spenser was still not sure what it was.

'Has anyone heard from Sonia at Woman's Action?' the boy with the red head-band asked, his mouth full.

'She brought round the final communiqué last night,' a girl answered. 'The meeting's tomorrow.'

'I see the fuzz have been out and about again. Islington this time.'

The conversation was held in a monotone, with long silences between each sentence. Spenser Spender hadn't the faintest idea what anyone was talking about and, since no one made any attempt to explain matters to him, he simply carried on eating. It was some kind of rice, with foul-tasting beans embedded in it. This was their world, he sensed, and it was assumed that everyone was part of it. Job Penstone looked on with parental benevolence. 'The Fascists,' he said after one particularly long silence, 'are planning to disrupt the Animal Rights meeting next month, or so our spies inform me. Any suggestions about a possible course of action?'

'We don't let the bastards in,' the red head-band muttered into his rice.

'But this is a democratic meeting, Peter. Don't use the enemy's tactics against the enemy.'

'Okay. We let them in and then we do them.'

'Do what to them?'

'Castrate them, the bastards,' The young woman had a thin, middle-class voice.

'So what are you into, squire?' Peter asked Spenser.

'I'm into films, actually.'

'What, with the underground cooperative?'

'No, actually not with that, I'm afraid. I'm making a film of *Little Dorrit* at the moment.'

'What's that when it's at home?'

'It's a novel. By Charles Dickens. You know, the...'

'Yeah, yeah. I get it.'

'I was reading about Dickens the other day,' the young woman began. 'You know he was anti-feminist, don't you?'

'I didn't actually.'

'Well, it's something you should think about. There are no women in his books – no real women, that is, just male stereotypes. How many women have you got working with you, anyway?'

'Jane has a point there, you know.' Job Penstone intervened, more quickly than seemed normal at this table. He looked at Spenser with a curious mixture of apology and defiance. 'Dickens's women are always pathetic, or pseudo-masculine, figures.'

'Isn't he the bloke on your course, Job?' This was a young man who had not, before, opened his mouth except to eat. 'The one fighting social injustice and for the rights of the working class?'

'Yes, that's right, Nick. You have it in one.'

'Well, it's a good cause then, mate.' Nick turned to Spenser. 'We need all the support we can get, with all these reactionary rat-bags in the government.'

Spenser Spender nodded, smiled and took refuge in his

plate of rice. He felt oddly threatened by this group of young people, and yet at the same time vaguely sympathetic towards them. Despite their foolishness, they had a point. Perhaps he would give the film more of a documentary look. He saw dark walls, he heard the sound of ancient and fearsome machinery. He would make sure that the human figures were continually being diminished by the noise and the spectacle of the city. His dinner had not been wasted, after all.

When the rice and beans had been eaten, and there was some talk of 'loosening up', whatever that meant, Spenser Spender apologised for taking up so much of Job Penstone's time actually. He had been a great help – he would let him know how things were getting along. Had he brought a coat with him, he couldn't remember?

He walked a few yards, while still in sight of the house, and then he began to run, sliding on the wet leaves under foot. His cheeks were burning – out of shame, embarrassment? – and the North London air felt cool upon them.

sixteen

Spenser had not, in a way, wanted to meet Rowan Phillips – but, at Sir Frederick Lustlambert's request, he had 'phoned him and had agreed to see him in Cambridge. Spenser did not want to be further confused: each time a new interpretation of *Little Dorrit* was sprung upon him, it subtly devalued his own and it took a conscious effort of will for him to reassert it. There was no doubt, though, that Phillips was the man for the script.

Rowan Phillips had agreed enthusiastically to the meeting, although he had kept his enthusiasm – like any of his more violent emotions – to himself. Dickens was, after all, his new 'area' and he saw also the prospect of money: the 'film world', as he thought of it, might be a fruitful source of income and also of prestige. He hadn't yet decided how to appear to Spenser Spender – as the academic blanching at the idea of scripts and cameras and actors but willing to be slowly won over, or as the professional novelist and critic at home in the 'media', brisk and self-confident, perhaps even slightly condescending. He had decided upon a refined version of the latter approach, but there was no reason why he should not also trade upon the former. That was why he had suggested Cambridge for their meeting. He had great faith in the social uses of history.

Spenser Spender decided to walk from the railway station, rather than hire a taxi. He was too early – it was his customary problem, but one which seemed to him to be incurable. The idea of leaving home later was not one he would consider sensible. But the directions he had been given to Rowan Phillips's college were vague ones, and he wandered through quaint, cobble-stoned alleys and over tiny bridges with an increasing sense of frustration. It was cold here, and these dark little streets seemed designed to confuse.

The whole place resembled a film set which had been left standing for too long. Students, who looked to him like schoolboys, rushed past with an air of furious concentration. The faces of these young men were as pale and weary as those of clerks in a large office complex.

He found, eventually, Rowan Phillips's college – it looked to Spenser to be merely a pile of dull stone, small, crouched, as if obsessed by something. A wizened creature, wearing an undertaker's suit, was watching him through a glass panel. 'And what bay you wanten, sir?'

'I have an appointment with Mr Phillips. My name is Spender.'

'Ah, Mr Spender, is it? Now let's bay taking a lawk in ere then shall we, sir?' The wizened creature leafed through what looked like an old newspaper, carefully and at great length. 'Here we bay. Kitchen Staircase, sir, second left then third on your raight. With all the oivy covering it, sir.' The creature's subservient manner was clearly some kind of joke: there was malice in that eye, cynicism in that accent, downright evil in his slowness.

Spenser Spender found the right door, knocked, and it seemed as though doors were being opened everywhere. A face on the same landing peered around an alcove to the left, and then disappeared abruptly. Someone else paused on the stairway and stared momentarily at Spenser. And then Rowan Phillips appeared, ushering Spenser into a room that seemed larger than the college itself. 'Ah, Mr Spender, it was good of you to come so far. So cold here, don't you think?' Rowan's voice had reverted to a slightly inflected English. Spenser Spender noticed that he was rather smartly dressed, that the clothes were somehow meant for looking at.

Rowan in his turn wondered if Spenser might be gay. It was his usual polite, mental enquiry to himself.

They sat down, at the same moment, at opposite ends of a dark sofa. Spenser misjudged its softness and sank too far within it. Rowan sat with his good profile forward, as if auditioning for a part in the film himself. Would Mr Spender, no please call me Spenser, would Spenser like a glass of sherry? It was a little early but, after all, why not? We academics have so few vices. Bright laughter from both parties as Rowan Phillips jumped up and disappeared inside a dark and voluminous cupboard, emerging some time later with a bottle and two glasses. Spenser studied the room: an old reading pulpit, a portrait of Dickens, a photograph of Auden which appeared to have been signed, leather volumes in piles upon a worn carpet.

'You know,' Rowan began on his return from the long voyage inside the cupboard, 'strangely enough, I was walking around Marshalsea only the other day – out of sheer curiosity, I suppose. Such interesting-looking people there, it seems to me. Had you any idea of using those old streets for your own purposes, Spenser?' He had rehearsed his opening lines, and he was word-perfect.

'I had, actually. There are certain parts of that district which would be just right, just old enough. And you know, with the Film Board, we're on a tight budget...' Rowan Phillips smiled and demurred, as if he knew such things already and took no account of them. In fact the news came as something of a shock. He had expected riches. '...Ar d so we need all the outside locations we can get. The good thing about the FFB – the Film Board, I mean—' Rowan smiled again, as if no explanation were necessary – 'is that they can persuade local councils to give us permission. Anyway, I like the idea of using some of the old streets.'

'Of course, of course. Some of them have changed remarkably little'

'You've done some work on Dickens, haven't you, actually?'

'I've been working on some academic stuff, if that's what you mean – symbols, you know, that sort of thing. I'm afraid you must find us academics terribly dull, terribly out of synch.' He used the expression as though it came naturally to him, although in fact he had never employed it before.

'No, not at all actually. I'm interested in symbols myself – in my work I live off them, in a way.'

Rowan Phillips was watching Spenser with great attention, but his eyes shifted away whenever Spenser looked at him. 'But I presume you were thinking more of my other work, my novels, when you contacted me?'

'Well, I was thinking of both, actually.'

'Ah yes. Both.'

'Yes, both. Dickens and fiction – they make a good pair, actually,'

'Well, he thought so too.'

Spenser was now too intent upon his subject to notice Rowan's little joke. 'No, I mean for the film script – hand in hand, you might say.' Rowan blushed, and got up from the sofa to pour two more glasses of sherry.

'It's an interesting project, Spenser,' he said with his back turned away from him. 'I see *Little Dorrit* really in terms of its symbolic structure, the ambiguity of its images. Although,' he added as he turned round and saw that Spenser's attention had not been fully held, 'this is the academic in me talking.'

'No, I'm interested in structure also, Rowan. I like the idea of a perfect structure – a refined version of the book.'

Rowan decided that this was the moment to become the moderately successful novelist. 'But if we're talking about a script, Spenser, I think these things would obviously be better left unsaid in it. We need to find a modern London vernacular, er, speech.' Rowan adjusted his sock – some flesh was showing just below the trouser leg. 'And the characters may have to say things which in the book Dickens says for them. Don't you agree?'

Yes, Spenser did agree; although he knew that any script which Rowan Phillips might produce would merely serve as a prompt-book for the dialogue as it emerged in the course of filming.

'Do you want voice-overs?' Rowan asked. It was a phrase he had picked up from the columns of the more knowing television critics.

'Voice-overs?'

'Well, I mean, do you want a narrator helping the action along? No, of course you don't. It's a novelistic device, of course it is.' He was flustered, and rearranged himself upon the sofa.

'I don't think it will be necessary, actually.'

'No, of course not.'

'I want to end the film, Rowan, when Little Dorrit and her father leave the Marshalsea after their debts have been paid.'

'Excellent. Novelistically speaking, that seems to me to be

the climax of the text, I mean book. That's excellent.'

'That's good, actually. You think there's a point in that?'

'Of course. Yes.'

Spenser Spender took out of his briefcase the scenario he had organised, breaking down the film sequence by sequence on small cards so that it resembled some kind of parlour game. Spenser was good at such things; he could have the skeleton of a film together without even knowing what the film was. He explained to Rowan that most sequences would need dialogue, and were marked accordingly, and the approximate time for each sequence was written down at the bottom of the card. He enjoyed his presentation to Rowan, since it suggested that everything was already ordered and defined. Of course it would be nice if Rowan, assuming he had the time, could work quite quickly. He really needed a rough version of the script in two months. It was very easy to do, Rowan would see. It wasn't like writing a novel or anything.

'Will you,' Rowan asked, 'be using any extras?'

'Extras?'

'You know, people who are used in crowd scenes and so on.'

'Oh, that kind of extra. Probably, yes. Why do you ask?'

'Well, it's just that some of those faces I saw in Marshalsea could have come straight out of Dickens – that pale, rather noble, look amongst the boys and of course the girls too. I'm sure the people there would be only too willing to help.' Rowan darted up again, as if shaking off what he had just said, and poured yet more sherry. He nodded at the portrait of Dickens on his wall – he had, in fact, placed it there the night before in a position normally reserved for a print by Mondrian. Previously, Dickens had been in the cupboard with the sherry.

'There he is looking down on us, Spenser, the greatest writer of his period. Don't you think? Even the greatest of all English novelists.' They toasted Dickens with their glasses of sherry, the two of them on the sofa, looking smart in their suits.

Rowan had asked Spenser to stay for dinner in hall. Spenser thought that he had said 'hole', or perhaps 'Hull'.

But his little Letty had said that she was going out anyway, and he had accepted the invitation. Now, as they toasted the portrait of Dickens, a series of deep bells sounded with a melodramatic flourish – as if Dickens were answering back. Rowan disappeared again into the cupboard, and came out with a black gown. He put it on with a certain élan, and automatically puffed out the sleeves. It was clear that he felt happiest in black.

'I'm afraid,' he said, looming over Spenser Spender, 'you may find all of this rather boring.'

With much making way for each other, after-you-ing and what a nice night-ing, they eventually made their way out of Rowan's room, across the courtyard, and into a large common room. Rowan introduced 'Mr Spender, the film director' to several other black gowns, who smiled and introduced him to someone else – he was, as it were, handed round.

Then, like a small migration of bats, they proceeded into hole or Hull, where the students were already standing and shuffling their feet and yawning. Spenser noticed that they had, in the mass, the same look as those inmates he had watched in the prison courtyard: quiet, passive, preoccupied. He thought of Pally again, lying on his bunk. Did he have any friends, or even relations, to visit him there?

Some foreign words were muttered and Spenser sat between two black gowns. The gowns began eating their food with considerable ferocity, kept their eyes upon their plates, and made no effort to speak to him. He looked up at Rowan, who sat opposite him, and Rowan looked quickly at the gown to Spenser's right. 'Mr Spender is making a film from Dickens's *Little Dorrit*, Howard. That's rather your area, isn't it?'

The gown looked up, having been startled into consciousness, turned to Spenser with a hurried movement and began talking – so quickly that Spenser could scarcely understand him. 'Goodness how extraordinary I was examining the text could you pass me a little more bread please how kind only the other day but it seems to me that the verbal associations without wishing to sound too pretentious are locked in as it were to a mode of discourse which do please correct me if you disagree I was reading an essay of Derrida's do you know his work yesterday at least I think it was yesterday—'

'Forgive my ignorance, Mr Spender—' the black gown on the other side of Spenser had started talking; he was, clearly, used to interrupting the black gown on the other side, who himself seemed used to being interrupted – 'Goodness me yes how silly of me to rabbit on Derrida is hardly the most interesting of topics even to me he lacks somehow a kind of—'

'I beg your pardon?' Spenser was saying.

'Forgive my ignorance, Mr Spender—' he said it so majestically that ignorance became a kind of virtue – 'but do you film people know how to anticipate popular taste? How do you measure it? How do you discern it? How do you, as it were, gauge it?'

'I'm afraid I don't. I just follow my nose.'

'Your nose, as it were?'

'Yes, my nose.'

'I'm afraid to say,' he carried on with majesty unimpaired by the mention of that protuberance, 'that I rarely go to the cinema these days.' It was as if the cinema were at fault for not insisting upon his presence.

'Oh, really? Well, you're not missing a great deal, just one or two good films.'

The black gown seemed a little nonplussed at Spenser's relative agreement.

'Should one learn to call it an art, Mr Spender?'

'I don't think it matters what you call it. But since we describe as art those things in which we generally take no interest, the name will do very well.'

The black gown paused, turned to his neighbour, and began discussing something else.

Spenser looked up at Rowan, who smiled and then blushed. God how boring it all is, thought Spenser, without Letty here.

seventeen

Although Laetitia had not formally 'moved in' with Andrew, she had been spending most of her time with him; he was continually attentive to her, especially when it came to sex. After years of self-induced privation – although, looking back on it, she could not be sure that Spenser had not acquiesced willingly in the situation – she found Andrew's love-making intense and gratifying. She rediscovered her own body in the process – instead of seeing it as the enemy, something she had to fight against with its colds and aches and sweatings, she saw it now as her real and proper self. It no longer frightened her, or gave her sudden surprises. She moved more easily, more freely, now.

It was this over-riding sensation of freedom which drew her to Andrew, but it was a feeling subtly complemented by the fact that she was now able to mix more self-confidently with other people. At first she had marvelled at Andrew's wide acquaintance, until she realised that this was the way that most people lived. And so she adjusted. She learned how to maintain a conversation without feeling that she was boring or stupid. She started saying what she felt, and discovered in the process that she could amuse people.

It seemed that the person she had been, and in fact still was, with her husband had been abandoned, or at least outpaced. She knew that she could not display her newly realised self with Spenser: he would find it unfamiliar and threatening. They would be strangers with each other. And yet she was determined not to lose these new discoveries she had made about herself – even if that meant leaving him altogether. Anyway, she said to herself in atonement, Spenser hardly saw her these days, he was so wrapped up in his film, and he wouldn't notice if she was gone. He had suspected nothing when she used her mother as an excuse for an uninterrupted week with Andrew, and she marvelled at his lack of interest. It was not fair on him, or on her – he would have to be told.

But she was not sure if this was her own decision, or Andrew's. It was his gift to see such things clearly. 'He just wants a body around, Letty my darling, to shop and clean for him while he gets on with his precious work.' Laetitia would nod thoughtfully and agree; she tried to think of Spenser in these terms.

'Have you told him about us yet, Letty?' Andrew would ask, almost every day. 'Does he know about me?'

'No, Andrew, I haven't told him yet. I never get the chance.' At such moments, Andrew would bite his lip and turn away from her. And Laetitia would say, 'But don't worry, Andrew. I will tell him. You know I love you more than I love him.' And Andrew would turn to her, take her in his arms, and call her his darling lover, always his own. At such moments, she knew she would be forced to act soon.

When Spenser returned home after dinner in Cambridge, he expected to find his Letty curled up in the nest asleep. The flat was in darkness; one of the heaters had broken, and Spenser felt a cold draught as he opened the door. He switched on a lamp, and found a note left upon his desk. It had been scrawled hurriedly, in capitals, like a lurid head-line: GONE OUT WITH A FRIEND. BACK LATER. No mention of 'love' or 'miss you'. In any case, it was not like Letty to go out so suddenly or quixotically – and, anyway, whom did she know distantly enough just to call 'a friend'? Come to think of it, she had been rather preoccupied lately. He assumed she was sickening for something, and had meant to ask her about it. The fact that he had not done so made him, for the first time, feel ill at ease.

He had let his eyes wander only over the surface of her life. He wanted to ask her about herself, he wanted to talk seriously with her about having a baby, for example, but, somehow, he could not confront her as a person – he would flinch at the sight, as though his eyes were in danger of being wounded. He loved her, as one would love a child; it was a safe love – he was comfortable within it. Any recognition of her as an equal human being would render him uncomfortable.

He was working on his notes, late into the night, when she came in. She seemed flushed from the cold.

'Hello, lettuce leaf, why are you home so late?'

'I've been out, Spenser.' She sounded abrupt and preoccupied, and Spenser turned back to his notes in order to hide within them. She sat down heavily upon a chair; after a minute, he looked up at her again.

'So where have you been Letty?'

'Just out. Out. Out. Out.'

She went through to the kitchen and filled the kettle. Spenser watched her as she stood at the sink, the kettle overflowing. She put it on to the stove without lighting it. She came back into the room.

'Spenser, I have to talk to you.'

'What about, lettuce leaf?'

'No, please be serious, Spenser. This is important.' She straightened a picture on the wall. 'I want to leave you.'

'What?'

'I want to leave you. I want to live with somebody else.' The words hardly seemed to affect him. He smiled at her.

'What are you talking about, Letty? You know we love each other.'

Laetitia sat down on the sofa, and began to cry.

'Don't cry, Letty, you know I love you. Don't cry.'

She looked at him hopelessly.

'I'm crying for you, Spenser, not for me. I'm crying for you.'

It was as if a large object had been hurled at him, knocking him against the wall. 'Oh Letty, what's happening to you?'

She opened out her arms to her husband. 'We never have sex or anything, and now I have to do this to you. I'm so sorry, so sorry.' He could feel Laetitia's tears on his cheeks as they embraced each other, but he did not feel like crying. He was watching his own reactions, analysing the situation. 'Don't cry, Letty. It'll be all right, you see. I'll be okay.' He did not in fact believe that she would actually leave him – that she would physically leave the flat. But then she very gently moved away from his arms, and went into the bedroom. She came out with a suitcase.

'I packed this two days ago,' she said, 'and you didn't even see it. Really you are the end sometimes.' She smiled at him and then went towards the door.

He had to speak to her, but he could think of nothing to say. And she could not say it for him. She walked across the room because that was, for weeks, what she had planned to do. He stared at her as she did so, watching her movements. He watched her walk to the door, open it, close it, walk up the stairs and into the street. There seemed to be no sound.

After she had gone, he continued looking out at the dark stairway. Then he got up and switched on the radio; he lit the burner beneath the kettle, sat in a kitchen chair and stared at the wall. His hands and feet were tingling and his face had gone numb, as though a cold wind were blowing into it. It was then that he started to cry; he laid himself down upon the floor and sobbed. In the process, he forgot exactly what it was he was crying about – he became just a body and a noise over which he had no control. There was nothing outside himself, no world; there was nothing inside himself.

He knew that he had behaved like this when his mother had abandoned him, that it was the memory of this which drew him back to the streets of his childhood, that it was the condition which he most dreaded and yet was most sure would be inflicted upon him. Letty had left him – *him*, a person called Spenser Spender – his baby had gone from him. He was the baby and his parent had left him. The two babies had gone. The two adults had left each other. He was a baby no longer. The bright, connected line which had been his past, and which connected him to the future, had snapped. His life was over.

The kettle was whistling now; he got up and poured the hot water into the teapot. He stirred the tea-bags, contemplating his own sense of isolation. He knew the sensations which would soon invade him – the loneliness, the self-pity, the paranoia which would prevent him from discussing such things with anyone, the helplessness and cringing insufficiency in the face of the world. Letty had walked away – he had made her do it. He had not loved her enough. He was an inadequate human being. He knew that he had felt such things before, but he did not want to think about that now.

He was still wearing his suit from the trip to Cambridge and, without thinking, he went over to the mirror in order to adjust the knot in his tie. He saw that his hands were shaking; he said over and over again to himself, 'Little Dorrit, Little Dorrit, Little Dorrit, Little Dorrit, Little Dorrit, Little Dorrit, Little Dorrit...'

eighteen

Audrey knew now that a plot was being hatched against her. She had telephoned Tim on a Sunday afternoon, and his mother told her that he was out seeing some foreigner. She didn't catch the name, but he had a funny accent, American sort of thing. Audrey knew who that was: it was that one, the writer who had been keen on Little Dorrit. He was a crafty one, asking her about the neighbourhood without so much as a by-your-leave. She had obviously stumbled upon some secret – perhaps Little Dorrit had buried some gold coins somewhere around here – and they wanted it from her. She wondered if they would use torture. That evening she had confronted Tim with her knowledge, but he denied it. He didn't know a thing, not one thing, about this Little Dorrit. But when he also denied having seen Rowan Phillips, he looked embarrassed and stroked his face. She knew he was lying, but she decided not to press home her advantage – it might come in useful later, this particular bare-faced lie.

At night now, after work, she would wander over the site of the old Marshalsea prison, looking for clues, some kind of old marks. She asked in the local stationers if the Victorians used chalk or not, and she bought an old map of the area which she would study without, in fact, knowing what she was looking for. She noticed for the first time that there were a great many plaques on the pubs and houses near her – 'As Commemorated in Charles Dickens's "Little Dorrit"' – and she would mark the spot with an 'X' on her map. When she got home, she drew lines between the 'X's, in case they formed a symbol, but all she got was a makeshift shape with five sides. Still, it was a start. She telephoned the medium in Ealing Common, Miss Norman, for further information about the girl who had spoken through her, but she received a non-committal reply. Miss Norman had no idea what kind of person the spirit guardian had sent; all types and classes made the journey from the other world, and you have to realise, my dear, that I can't work miracles. Not even for my regulars.

Meanwhile, Tim had had gone to his doctor, as Rowan had suggested, and described someone – a friend of his, really – who was feeling sort of peculiar. The doctor assumed that Tim was talking about himself and, being a busy man, briskly wrote out a prescription for some mild tranquillisers without asking any questions. Tim had not known what to do with them, so he put them in a drawer at home. His father started taking them from time to time, thinking they were aspirin, and felt much better for it.

Tim still saw Audrey, but she scarcely paid any attention to him. He had loved her, and now he was being given the cold shoulder. He had never felt the same way about any other girl, but his hopes of perpetual comfort, of happiness, of 'going steady', were being dismantled in front of him. He went swimming every day, pounding through the water grim-faced, completing lap after lap; he had even begun to time himself with a stopwatch. It was a way of keeping a bit of control, he said to himself. One afternoon he left the watch by the side of the pool, and it was stolen. For the first time in years he cried, and then jumped in the water so that no one could see his tears.

He went to see Audrey that night. She had given him the watch last Christmas, and he wanted to tell her that it had been stolen. But, when he explained what had happened, she simply laughed and said mysteriously, 'We all lose the thing we love.' Then she turned upon him with ferocity. 'I should know that, shouldn't I?' Tim looked puzzled. 'Why don't you admit you're trying to cheat me. Go on then, admit it.' 'Cheat you, Aud?' 'Yes, cheat. C, h, e, a, t.' He did not understand her any more, and looked down at the burn in the carpet. 'You and that so-called writer of yours.' She had the strange clarity of the possessed: 'You'll be next. It won't stop with me. It never does, does it? They want all of us.' He tried to put his arm round her, to still her, to prevent her from shaking, from talking. She brushed him aside. 'Oh, don't look all gooey-eyed at me, Timothy Coleman. Why don't you just go and get your arse out of here?' She switched on the television: a club near Oxford Street had been hit by incendiary bombs. No one had got out alive. Audrey watched the scene greedily; she had forgotten already that Tim was still in the room.

He looked at his hands for a moment, turning them over and over as if they were the hands of a stranger, and then without looking at Audrey let himself quietly out of the flat. Without thinking about what he was doing, he walked across the street and stared into the nearest shop window. It belonged to an old-fashioned 'Magic Shop', and Tim looked carefully at the whoopee cushions, the nail-through-the-finger trick, the false-bottomed glass and the grinning, devilish masks. For some reason, he grinned back; or, rather, he screwed up his face so that it resembled a mask.

He felt exhausted now, in need of a drink. He walked to the pub in which he had been with Rowan Phillips. He stood by the bar and drank with a kind of nervous exasperation – with the same concentration he might give to biting his nails. The alcohol affected him almost at once, and he leaned against the bar. He took out his wallet, and Rowan Phillips' number was there inside it, on a slip of paper. He stared at it, as if the name were unfamiliar. But Rowan was a friend; he was a mate; he understood what Tim was going through; he was someone to rely on, to talk to.

He went to the telephone booth in the corner of the pub, and dialled the number. He was brimming over with words, the words he had suppressed with Audrey, and he did not wait for Rowan to speak when he picked up the receiver. 'Hello, mate, this is Tim here. Do you remember me then? How are you feeling?'

'I'm fine, Tim. Of course I remember you, I'm just fine.'

'Well, I just felt like a bit of a natter. It's cold tonight, isn't it? Real monkeys.'

'Yes, it is cold, Tim.'

'Do you feel like coming out for a drink then, mate? If you're at a loose end, like.'

'I'd love to, Tim, but it is a bit late.' Rowan had managed to recover from his initial surprise. 'Why don't you come over here – I've got some whisky and some beer.'

'Okay then, mate, I wouldn't say no to another one, I'll

grant you that. Where are you then exactly?' Tim wrote down the address laboriously, and then went back to the bar to order another drink.

Rowan, meanwhile, hurried out to the off-licence in order to buy the whisky and beer he was supposed to have. He refused to consider the implications of the call: it might be that Tim was with some friends, and would bring them with him. He sounded tipsy, anyway. He would have to be careful.

At closing time, Tim left the bar with the stiff walk of someone trying not to draw attention to his own drunkenness. He had almost forgotten his call to Rowan – it was only when he anticipated the scene at his parents' house, staggering through, knocking things down, slurring his speech, that he remembered that Rowan had asked him over for a drink. He took out his wallet and scrutinised the address; he was swaying slightly in the cold wind outside. He saw a taxi, hailed it, and gave the driver the piece of paper.

Rowan had decided to have a bath. He put on his jeans and a clean T-shirt, but then he changed his mind and put on an ordinary shirt. He did not want to seem too eager. Perhaps he ought to adopt the role of the father-figure rather than the friend. He didn't smoke, in case it made his breath smell; he had a whisky, instead. One hour later, his excitement had turned to frustration and then to anger – Tim was just having a laugh at his expense. He was a drunken yob. Rowan kept on drinking. He would go to a club, and pick someone up. Tim could go to hell.

When the front-door bell rang, so long that someone must have been leaning against it, Rowan jumped out of the chair. He went instinctively to the mirror, unbuttoned his shirt and then buttoned it up again. When he opened the door, Tim almost fell inside.

'Hello, Rowan, old mate, I'm glad to see you again, I really am.'

'Hi, Tim, come on in and sit down.' He guided Tim to the sofa.

'How's my old mate then, are you okay. How's the writing coming on then, mate?' Tim was falling slightly to one side.

'It's just fine, Tim. Have you had a good time tonight?' Tim, ruddy with drink and the cold, looked picturesque to

Rowan, who crossed and then uncrossed his legs. He thought of Alcibiades, flushed with wine.

'I've just been drinking with some mates, Rowan, just some mates. I saw Audrey tonight, to speak of the devil.'

'Oh, yes. How was she?'

'Oh, pretty much the same like, Rowan, pretty much the same.' Tim flopped down upon the sofa, perhaps preparing for sleep. It was so out of character that Rowan felt emboldened: he might be able to act out of character, also.

'Do you feel like a drink, Tim?'

'I wouldn't say no, Rowan. Ta very much.'

Tim drank greedily, like a child. 'Audrey thinks you're queer, Rowan. Are you queer?'

'I don't know. Sometimes, I suppose. I told you I was bisexual.' Rowan wondered if there would ever come a time when he would stop lying about his sex life.

'I've never been queer, Rowan old mate. Did I tell you about my mate at school? He was queer, right, but he was a good mate, do you know what I mean like?' Rowan said that he did; he was slightly apprehensive, and at the same time excited.

'You've got to do what a man's got to do. Right, Rowan?'

Tim stretched out on the sofa, his legs apart, and looked up at the ceiling. Rowan, for once unwilling to think of the consequences of his action, knelt down beside Tim and unzipped his fly. Tim was saying, 'No don't, Rowan, don't. I'm straight. Don't.' But his cock was erect, and he made no effort to stop Rowan sucking it. When he came, he propped himself up on one elbow and looked at Rowan. 'Well, was that okay for you? Do you enjoy doing that to blokes?' He seemed to have sobered up, and the flush had gone from his cheeks. Then he started to cry; Rowan, nonplussed, struggled up from his kneeling position and put his hand on Tim's shoulder. Tim was muttering something about a watch and seeing Audrey. He grasped Rowan's arm and pulled him towards him, and held him as a man holds on to a fixed object during a gale. It was as if his life itself were in danger of being blown away.

PART TWO

nineteen

Spring had arrived in London, apparently by accident. Like frozen food which is suddenly placed upon a warm plate, the city seemed to melt at the edges. At seven o'clock one Sunday morning, Spenser Spender was standing by the Thames, which seemed curiously light and fast-moving in the early morning; Spenser was talking to a very tall woman who was wearing a bonnet and was clad in an indistinguishable mound of clothes – she resembled a pile of laundry which had come suddenly to life. 'Close your mouth a bit more,' he was saying to her, 'so that the words are forced out.' She nodded briefly; any extravagant movement might bring the laundry down around her. 'And don't let your eyes move so much – keep them fixed on something. Actually, just fix them on me. I'll be just behind the camera. So fix them on me.'

Three green trailers were parked beside one of the many disused warehouses which turn the banks of the Thames into a series of damp and musty caves, full of echoes and sudden movements. Some men in green overalls were taking large arc-lights from the back of one of the trailers; cables lay along the narrow street which separated the river from the warehouse alongside it. To one side, a heavy black canvas was being hoisted above the heads of the actors and of the crew, effectively blocking out the rising sun. The arc lights were now being pointed towards the canvas; when they were turned on, the effect was one of brilliant gloom. An incandescent darkness was laid upon the waters and the dilapidated buildings – later, in the studio, Spenser hoped to make it darker still.

He had been filming now for six weeks, mainly on interior sets, and he had completed much of the essential narrative work. It turned out that the melodramatic elements had been essential to the story of *Little Dorrit*, and Spenser had decided to make a cinematic virtue out of necessity by emphasising the theatrical, almost caricatured, elements in the plot. Rowan Phillips's script had been serviceable, a useful aid. He had simplified the plot and retained the language, as Spenser had instructed. He had produced a skeleton which Spenser was now busy disguising, using his actors and his cameras as the multi-coloured cloths of his design. He had not yet filmed the prison sequences, nor had he done any sustained work on location. These two aspects of the film – the prison and the city – were the ones which would lend it atmosphere and authority. He pondered over them late into the night, keeping his mind continually engaged to keep it from slipping back into memories of Letty. This Sunday morning, he felt tense and anxious, his mood in almost comic contrast to the relaxed and often jovial manner of the crew who surrounded him. For them it was a day's work; for him it was now his life.

Two members of the crew were painting the narrow road itself with a kind of black wash, black right up to the river's edge. The railings were coated in golden paint, which would appear as brass upon the screen. The warehouses were also being quickly covered with a dull greyish paint, making what was dismal more dismal still.

Three women sat on chairs behind the camera: the laundry pile and two others. One was a small, thin woman who sat with her hands clenched tightly between her legs; she was biting her lip with such ferocity that she might have been trying to eat herself for breakfast. The other, a rather fat middle-aged woman in a faded black dress, was shouting something at the cameraman perched some feet in the air like a crow about to swoop on some crumbs. He smiled at her and raised his thumb. She winked and roared with laughter. Against one of the warehouses sat a group of about a dozen men, all in poses of self-conscious tiredness, all nondescriptly dressed in grey or brown. They were making caustic remarks about the three women, the set, the time of day, and Spenser himself.

The arc lights had now been arranged in a half-circle so as to shine directly upon the Thames itself, illuminating its interior like an aquarium. Spenser wandered over to the three women, and squatted down beside their chairs. Then he got up, said something to an assistant, who in turn said something to the cameraman. The noise of the crew was beginning to subside. The three women walked towards the railings beside the river – the laundry pile positioned herself to the left of a chalk mark, the thin and fat women to the right. These two faced each other like a miniature tragic chorus, while the laundry pile looked out over the water, now brightly lit. The heavy cloth above the set and the freshly painted road lent to the scene an artificial darkness which would have disturbed or puzzled the senses of anyone coming across it by chance.

Spenser walked up to the two women facing each other, and turned the thin one on her axis like a mannequin in a shop-window. He walked back and stood behind the camera. 'Quiet please, everyone. Right, off we go.'

A young man appeared with a small board, almost tripping over one of the cables in his nervousness. 'Action!' The fat woman took one step back and began talking.

'Why, you're a woman!'

'Don't mind that,' the thin one replied and moved one step towards her. She took her hand. 'I'm not afraid of you.'

'Then you had better be. Have you no mother?'

'No.'

'No father?'

'Yes, a very dear one.'

'Then go home to him and be afraid of me. I never should have touched you but I thought you were a child.'

'Cut!'

The three women walked at once back to their chairs. Spenser peered through the lens of the large camera. The arc-lights burned like a furnace, creating vivid shadows and giving a two-dimensional character to every object that they illuminated. On a signal from Spenser, the three women moved once again towards the railings – 'And, Jennifer,' he said to the fat one, 'could you move a little bit more. You're in distress – shake a little bit, as if someone is about to hit you.'

And so the same conversation was repeated, over and over.

The voices seemed absurdly thin as they rose into the morning air, as if taking flight from the crew who surrounded the actresses in a semi-circle and who watched them with an air of affected uninterest. They seemed only to come to life again when the scene was complete, when Spenser nodded to his assistant and the assistant nodded to the cameraman. It was in the can, right? The cameraman nodded gravely back. Everyone lined up for coffee, which was being poured from a large, electrically-heated urn.

The black canvas was hoisted up even higher above the set, and several smaller canvas awnings were placed in position beside it, in order to create darkness where there had been none before. Black felt was tacked into place along the narrow alley between the warehouses, and the sides of the vast and empty buildings had been coated in grey paint. Spenser Spender supervised the work, alternately looking through the camera which was now pointed away from the river and towards the warehouses. They rose in front of him like houses of darkness, oppressive and yet unreal. They had been transformed into replicas of warehouses. Reality itself had been suspended.

Everything was now complete. The scene was to be of night-life by the river, and it was to connect with the brief meeting and dialogue which had just been filmed. It was for this scene that the small band of extras had been hired. Spenser showed them, each one at a time, where they should stand, where they should move. He had envisioned a landscape like that of a dream, full of shouts, stray cries and sudden movements. The camera would track backwards, gradually taking in the whole area.

The extras took up the positions assigned to them, with a leisureliness that bordered upon cynicism. One or two of them had already complained about their rough and non-descript costumes – Spenser had decided that 'period' dress would be out of place, and so their clothes were deliberately drab and ambiguous. 'Okay, boys, are you in position?' They were. The young man with the clapperboard came out, gingerly stepping over the cables. 'Action!'

Some of the extras sauntered across the alley; two were to be seen in the right-hand corner in an intense and whispered conversation; a young man ran across the set, stopped, half-turned and let out a low and prolonged whistle. The camera moved backwards and upwards, and another man peered down from a small bridge which connected two warehouses – the man looked small and furtive, some forgotten inhabitant of the area. Just then the siren of a fire-engine, or perhaps a police car, sounded in a street nearby. 'Oh shit! Cut!'

The scene was repeated five times, with slight changes of movement and direction, until the performers themselves were in a daze. But as it developed it became clear to Spenser Spender, if to no one else, that it had a quality of intensity which could be reproduced upon the screen. He saw the darkness of the scene as an effective counterpoint to the glare coming off the river; the three women would be surrounded by movement and madness.

By now a group of residents had gathered close to the set in order to watch the action, behind a rope which had been hastily set up. The local council had agreed to guard the set when it was not being used, although Spenser had not expected anyone to arrive so early in the morning. But a small knot of interested parties had come to watch the area which they had known from their childhood converted into something which now resembled a cardboard toy. They were discussing the fat actress, who was again winking and smiling at the cameraman. 'Who's she when she's at home? I know the face but I can't put a name to it,' one elderly lady was saying to a balding middle-aged man who had a Sunday newspaper rolled up in his pocket. 'She looks as if she's been on the bottle she does. What are they doing here anyway on a Sunday morning? What they filming?'

'It's Little Dorrit. They've come to film Little Dorrit.' They turned round to see a red-haired woman leaning over the rope, restrained by it against her will. It was Audrey. She was watching the movements of the actors and crew with great attention; and, with a hungry look, she inspected the thin young actress. When she had been performing in front of the camera, Audrey had involuntarily put her hand in front of her mouth. She could not hear what was being said, but she knew that this was Little Dorrit. It had to be her.

As the camera crew started dismantling the lights and rolling up the cables, Audrey ducked under the rope and quickly walked up to the small group of actresses. The thin one had lost her nervous concentration, and was laughing at a remark which the fat one had just made. 'Oh Jennifer darling,' Audrey heard her say as she walked towards them, 'how can you be so monstrous to that lovely man? It's really unfair of you.' Audrey went up to her, quite boldly, as if she owned the place. 'Here, are you Little Dorrit?'

The thin one looked at her with a trace of annoyance. 'Well, I was, my dear, for a few minutes at least.' Jennifer laughed.

'Well, I'll tell you something else. You don't behave like her.' And then Audrey slapped the thin actress across the face. Before anyone could adequately take in this little incident, and before the thin actress had time to recover her composure, Audrey had gone down one of the alleys which led away from the river.

Audrey had heard about the film from Tim, who had naturally heard about it from Rowan Phillips. Tim was not himself interested in the matter, but now found himself in a position where he felt bound to placate both Rowan and Audrey in equal measure. He found the situation difficult to comprehend, let alone deal with. But, like a prisoner waking up each morning in the same cell, he saw no way out of his predicament which would not cause even more unpleasantness and retribution. And so the benevolence which, in the past, he had carried like a shield degenerated into a kind of passivity, a defencelessness which, in a less civilised environment, would have at once attracted predators.

He remembered very little about that first night with Rowan; the next morning, he woke in a strange bed, with Rowan snoring beside him. He felt crushed, broken; he wanted to creep out of this house silently. But Rowan woke; he turned, stared at Tim, and then smiled weakly. They both then avoided looking at each other.

'How are you feeling, Tim?'

'I'm okay, thanks. Got to get going though. I'll be late for work if I don't get a move on.' Rowan put his head back on the pillow and closed his eyes, preparing again for sleep. He might have been ready to dismiss Tim like the after-image of a dream; when he woke, he would be gone. Tim lay back on the bed. He felt lost, helpless. Audrey had abandoned him and now Rowan, the person to whom he had told everything, might also turn away. In such circumstances, the need to survive in other people's affections becomes the most pressing need of all. 'I'll tell you what, Rowan,' Tim said to the ceiling, 'I'll come round tonight if you like. For a drink, like.' The idea of drink actually made him gag. But Rowan did not notice; he put his hand on Tim's arm. 'That would be nice, Tim. Why don't we do that?' In such brief conversations are lives made and broken.

And so a routine emerged. Rowan spent the weekends, and Monday night, in London. Tim would come around one of those evenings; they would talk, have a few drinks, and then Tim would allow Rowan to 'blow' him, as Rowan called it. Tim thought the word ought to be 'suck' but he said nothing. In fact neither of them mentioned the event, before or after it occurred. Afterwards they would sleep in the same bed, but without sexual contact. Tim would get up, early, and go home or straight to work. Rowan would wake much later, pleased to have slept with Tim and glad now to be alone. It was in some ways a curiously impersonal relationship, and so it suited him very well. Tim simply found it bewildering; his life had veered out of control, and he was now in the position of being an observer of it rather than a participant. He did not particularly enjoy the sex with Rowan but then, on the other hand, he did not actively dislike it. He felt that he was in some way cheating Rowan by giving him so much pleasure for such little effort – at least on Tim's part.

But he enjoyed their conversations, as Rowan did. Because the most important things could not be discussed – most of them centring around the blowing or sucking, and sex in general – they were forced continually to act as strangers towards each other and, in such roles, they could talk quite freely about everything else. They were permanently on a train, speeding towards some unknown and unthinkable destination. Rowan told Tim about Canada, about Cambridge, and about his work on the film. Tim told Rowan about his job at the printers, about his family, about his schooldays.

About their present situation, they did not speak. If they had, Tim would have told Rowan that now, somehow, he felt closer to Audrey. She had represented everything that was familiar to him – everything, in fact, which was familiar in himself – before she had 'changed'. But now Tim, himself, had suffered a kind of change also. They had both, as it were, slipped out of gear. And so Tim made a point of visiting her, on Sunday afternoons and Wednesday evenings. Audrey put up with these visits, although she made no real effort to entertain Tim. The idea of sex was clearly repugnant to her – although for that Tim blamed himself. He thought that, somehow, she had guessed what was happening between him and Rowan and that she wanted nothing more to do with that side of him. He suffered this meekly, as a punishment for a sin. They would sit together, perhaps drawing strength from each other, Audrey sometimes in an excited and distracted mood, sometimes mournful and contemplative.

Their staple topic of conversation had become the film. When Tim first told Audrey about it, he simply pretended that he had heard a rumour in the pub. But she had jumped up and, although it was still only twilight, had pulled the curtains. 'So they're going to take a look at it, are they? Come nosing round here and get their hands on it all, are they?' Tim was surprised by the violence of her reaction – he thought that she would be pleased to hear of a film about her Little Dorrit – and determined never to mention the subject again. But she would not let the matter rest, and continually badgered him for further information. When he told her, rather hesitantly, that he thought that writer bloke was doing the script, she turned on him in a fury: 'Oh so he thinks he can get away with it too, does he? He thinks he can pick on Little Dorrit, does he? Well, she's too clever for him. Tell that to your fancy friend – she's too clever by half!'

But in subsequent days her anger seemed to subside, and was replaced by quiet but persistent curiosity. How far had they got? Where were they doing it? And who was acting Little Dorrit? In the face of these questions, Tim would turn

112

to Rowan for information. Sometimes Rowan would show Tim part of his script; Tim would stare at it with a dazed reverence, but made no effort to read it. He did not notice, for example, that Rowan was using phrases and expressions which he had picked up from Tim himself.

On the Sunday afternoon, after the filming had begun by the river, Tim paid his customary visit to Audrey. She greeted him in a great state of excitement: 'I showed them they can't get away with it, those clever ones. That cat pretending to be Little Dorrit – I saw her off good and proper. I just marched up to her and told her so.'

'Told her what, Aud?'

'That she wasn't worth the candle, that's what. She ought to know better, that one. If Little Dorrit saw what was going on she'd have a fit she really would.'

It was now firmly established in Audrey's mind that Little Dorrit was a real person – dead, probably, or she wouldn't have taken her over at the seance. It might be something to do with reincarnation, she wasn't exactly sure. Or perhaps Little Dorrit had known Audrey when Audrey was a little girl. Anyway, she knew that Little Dorrit had some message to pass on – perhaps it was about jewels or a lost inheritance. Something important. Audrey knew also that the others, the clever ones, wanted to get hold of the secret. That was why they had brought their big lights and cameras to search the area. At certain times, when her paranoia reached the stage of panic, Audrey would become Little Dorrit. She would kneel on the floor, and pray for her father and herself, pray to God that they would reap their just reward and that it would not be taken from them.

At work, her behaviour was exciting more comment. On some days, she seemed quite chatty and more what the girls described as her old self; on others she would stay in a kind of daze, staring ahead of her, answering only one call in three. One day she came in whistling, with her hands clenched beside her; this was a bad sign, and Margery did all she could to take her mind off things. She was chatting about these new birth control pills, and how you couldn't trust them, not definitely, that number is unobtainable, sir, thank you, when

Audrey started trying to open her console with a nail-file. She had unscrewed part of it and was fishing around at the circuits inside when then there was a small explosion and Audrey fell backwards. She was not hurt, although her hair seemed slightly singed, but the whole exchange was suddenly, to outside callers, unobtainable. When the supervisor asked her what she thought she was up to, she smiled at him and said she wanted to discover how it all worked.

The supervisor called some of the girls in. They all agreed that Audrey couldn't help herself, but there was a screw loose somewhere and it wasn't in the console. The supervisor was generous in his listening, grave in his deportment, anxious that the best thing be done. Steps would clearly have to be taken – he didn't know what steps yet, just steps. They would have to talk to the union, of course, before any definite decision was made.

Audrey knew nothing of such matters; at the time she was sitting in front of the now repaired board, singing as she worked. The words had occurred to her by chance, and she had made up a little tune to go with them:

> Who bleeds in the yard?
> Always she!
> Whose life is marred?
> Always me!

When she sang, her voice lost the shrillness which it often now had in conversation; it became surprisingly deep and resonant, as though she had been joined by someone else.

twenty

Sometimes Laetitia would set out on long walks through the streets of London; she would stare at the faces of the people she passed as if they contained some secret of life which she might summon up within herself. She passed shops which had banks of television sets in their windows, each with the same image. And then she would look in the windows of travel agents and airline offices, just to confirm that the world was open and free.

She had been living with Andrew for four months now, and was no longer sure about her own new freedom which she had obtained at such cost. It seemed that, as soon as she left Spenser, Andrew himself, who had instigated the break, nagging her into it almost daily, began to lose some of the interest he had shown in her. He would play his disco records, dancing by himself in the small front room as if she were not present; he would spend hours on the telephone talking to people whom she did not know. They would argue loudly and fiercely over trivial matters – although, in truth, she did not mind the arguments so much as the neglect. Andrew himself was changing. He seemed to be regarding her as simply another of his many social talents; he would advise her on her clothes and make-up, she might have been a doll he had himself invented and designed. Even if they had had, or were still having, a terrible row he would lead her out into the world of clubs and restaurants, of back-stage chats after a show, of parties, as if nothing whatsoever had happened. 'Marigold love,' he would say, 'you were really great tonight. Have you met Letty? You two are going to be really good friends.' It seemed to Laetitia that there was very little difference between herself and all the other women whom Andrew kissed, embraced and complimented – except that she was sleeping with him. And she was not even sure that this was her unique privilege any more.

And so her newly-found freedom turned to confusion and disappointment; she missed Spenser, she realised that. She missed their intimacy and their companionship. Andrew offered instead only what he called a 'fun time'. Laetitia started making excuses simply to get out of Andrew's flat – just to be on her own. Andrew sometimes became angry and suspicious when she remained out for a whole afternoon; it seemed to her that he was angry only because he had lost his audience.

Reflections such as these occurred fitfully to her as she walked through London at the beginning of spring. She found herself attracted to tall, dark streets where the new season had for some reason been refused entry. And yet the streets seemed to spawn life: she had never before realised quite how many people surrounded her in the course of her own daily activities. It was only when she, as it were, dropped out, and wandered without direction or purpose, that the fullness of the city presented itself to her. On one corner a young man – like a tramp, she thought, but so young to be one – played a tuba, its notes as wild and discordant as the life which passed by him.

Without thinking what she was doing, Laetitia entered a telephone box and dialled her old number. She expected Spenser to be there, although she had no idea what to say to him if he answered the 'phone. But he did not; Laetitia could imagine the sound of the 'phone as it rang through the empty flat. She could see the rooms themselves clearly now. She was, as it were, their vanishing point. Spenser had not even tried to contact her in the past three months; there had been no letters about divorce or solicitors, none of the plaintive demands she had expected. Perhaps he was simply waiting for her to return – and here her new-found instinct for liberty rose up within her and astonished her with its anger – and, then again, perhaps he had just forgotten her. She had ceased to exist for him when she had walked out of the flat.

She left the telephone booth and, on an impulse, hailed a taxi. When she arrived at her destination, she looked tentatively out at her old street in case she saw somebody she knew:

she felt like an impostor. She walked down the steps to the basement flat quietly and carefully; she peered through the window as a stranger might. She still had the key in her bag. She opened the door and called out, her voice unnaturally high, 'Spenser? Are you there, Spenser?' No sound; only the vague hum of the refrigerator. She walked through the flat: neat, precise, ordered, as though a murder had been committed and the flat had been sealed in order to await further examination. She took out a tissue, blew her nose, and flushed the tissue down the lavatory. She did not want to touch anything, or mar the order which Spenser had imposed.

She took out a piece of paper and wrote upon it, 'Spenser. Called round to see how you were. Letty.' She put it on Spenser's typewriter and let herself out of the flat. Halfway down the street, she stopped, turned back, went into the flat, and removed the note. When she got back into the street, she looked around and tore the note into pieces, dropping them down the nearest drain. She was terrified now of seeing Spenser accidentally, and walked quickly down side streets to Sloane Square tube station.

When she returned to Andrew's flat, she felt tired, almost without feeling. He was lying on the floor listening to disco music, played very loudly.

'Where have you been, Lettuce darling?'

'I went for a walk, Andrew. You know I can't stand being cooped up in here all day.'

'Oh do I bore you? I'm sorry, I hadn't realised that. Did you pick up any nice young men on the streets, dear?'

'If you really want to know, I went back to the flat to pick up some things.'

'And was dear Spenser there to hold your hand?'

'No. He wasn't there.'

Andrew began twitching his foot out of time with the music. He got up and began to dance around Laetitia, in some ritual preliminary, perhaps, to cooking and eating her.

'I suppose Spenser would love to have you back. Is that right? He's been crying in his beddy-bed-bed for you, right? He wants you to hold his hand, and his cock, while he's working. Is that right? God, you're such a weak lady, Laetitia. You can be so weak sometimes.'

'I told you. He wasn't there.' And now she became angry, the anger welling up in her by accident. 'And I suppose I should spend all my time with you, being introduced at parties and having to smile at your fucking idiot friends.'

'My friends are not idiots. They are talented, exciting people. If you find them idiotic, that's your problem. Some of them rather like you, as it happens.'

'Thanks for nothing.'

Andrew was looking at his face in the mirror, and stroking his beard. 'Well, let's not argue, Letty. Please. Anyway, I want to ask you a favour.'

'What is it now?'

'I want you to go and see your doctor.'

She looked at him, alarmed. 'Whatever for?'

'It's nothing serious. I've got some kind of discharge, you know what I mean. Venereal. It's all right, I've had it before. But I don't want our precious Lettuce catching anything from me, do I?'

'Do you mean to say you've given me venereal disease?' Someone had just punched her.

'I just want you to go for a check-up. It's not serious anyway. There's no need to get prima donnaish about it.'

'So I have to go and see my doctor. Is that right?'

'Yes, your doctor, Laetitia. He will give you some tablets. And that will be that.'

'That's it, is it? I've got venereal disease, and he gives me tablets.'

'Don't go on about it, Laetitia. You don't have to go, you know. I'm only doing you a favour.'

'You give me VD, and you're doing me a favour?'

'Let's drop this subject, shall we, Laetitia. It's beginning to bore me now. Forget I mentioned it to you.'

'So who did you catch it off?'

'I don't know. I could have had it for months. I could have got it off you. Anyway, let's drop it, shall we?'

She felt sick; the well of her body had been poisoned by some crawling, growing thing. She might have had it for months, this thing inside her, disfiguring her, eating her away. She wanted to vomit, but then she thought she might see signs of it there.

Andrew was running a bath, and singing loudly over the sound of the water. She knew that she could not go on living this way – the emptiness and the pointlessness of it all were like a physical force which robbed her of her strength. It seemed to her, at this moment, that her new identity was made of some fragile material which could not withstand shock of any kind. She hated Andrew – she felt that now, the feeling rising from the depths of herself – but she could not go back to Spenser Spender. She was entirely alone.

'Letty dear,' Andrew called from the bathroom, 'Joan has asked us to dinner tomorrow night. She's got some new boy-friend she wants us to meet. Isn't it a hoot? I said yes for us.'

Laetitia sat down on the worn sofa, and stared at this strange place she was in.

twenty-one

Spenser Spender had not been at home when Laetitia had called because he was back in the prison. The wing in which the film was to be shot had been abandoned about fifteen years before, because of its uncomfortable proximity to the prison wall. In the Fifties and early Sixties, there had been a number of famous escapes: Spenser could still remember the panic in the neighbourhood. He had been called in from the street, or brought in from the garden; the windows were barred and the doors bolted. And so, after much public pressure, the wing had been closed.

Now it was a perfect setting for Marshalsea – although constructed on different, and in fact harsher, principles than the old debtors' prison, the Victorian design perfectly suited Spenser's vision of decaying and repressive authority. There seemed to be one or two small holes in the roof through which birds flew in and out, their stray whistling quite out of place in this otherwise silent world of metal stairways and small, empty cells.

Spenser had decided to crowd the wing with actors and extras, with women and small children, so that there was both noise and bustle. Prisoners would visit one another's cells, food would be cooked on the landings, children would play ball-games against the walls of the wing – while, stretching above them, the bright lights, the walls painted in dark green, the thick bars at the windows and the metal landings, would emphasise their loss of freedom. The street scenes in London had been going well, and he wanted to contrast the rough and open life of the city with the bright but enclosed life of that city's debtors – its victims.

The prison inmates had heard about the film, but they treated the matter with the same mute lack of interest as they treated anything else which emerged from 'outside'. Some of them, however, were watching from the windows of their cells as the green trailers parked in the prison yard. Spenser Spender was already there, waiting for the crew, and he could see one or two of the prisoners' faces, as small and as pale as old coins, watching through the bars. But he was too busy supervising the unloading of the equipment to pay any attention to them. There were cables to be unrolled, lights to be set up, cameras to be prepared, the electrical paraphernalia of film-making all to be hooked up to the electrical generators underneath the prison itself.

There were two scenes which Spenser Spender wanted to complete on this first day. One was a long and inclusive shot of the Marshalsea Prison: the camera would pan upwards, taking in landing after landing, acting as a frame for the confused and noisy life of the inmates. The other scene would be between Little Dorrit and her father; he collapses and, in the moment of physical suffering and peril, faces the truth about himself which he has concealed for so long.

The actors, and the extras, had arrived on a special bus, and were milling around the entrance to the old wing; they fell silent as they entered the building itself. There was a curious, musty smell about the place which immediately impressed itself upon the performers. Spenser lost no time in arranging for the equipment to be set up, and for the actors to familiarise themselves with their new setting. During the course of the morning, the first scene gathered momentum and authority. Spencer moved from one 'take' to another until the actors understood what was required of them: on command, they would mimic the life of a noisy and helpless community, moving quickly, hesitantly, solemnly. As they walked across the central area of the prison, or banged their cell doors, or ran up and down the metal staircases, to prearranged signals, a tremendous shout rang out. The landings shook under their feet, and the cries and noises echoed around the old building, sending the small birds screaming out through the roof. It was as if all the ghosts of the prison had risen up together, creating that bright, unearthly light which shone from the wing and corrupted the daylight outside.

For the next scene, Little Dorrit was dressed in the dowdy

grey costume which she had worn before, by the river; but now its symbolism was obvious. It was a kind of prison costume, worn in homage to the inhabitants of this place. At the appropriate moment, the small, thin actress moved quickly through the crowd of inmates – who dispersed at once to make room for the camera which was following her as she walked swiftly towards her father, who had had a seizure. He lay propped up against the wall; the camera stopped as she stopped, and moved to the left to catch both of them within the same frame. The father speaks first.

'What does it matter whether I die here or not – now, next week, next year? What am I worth to anyone?'

Little Dorrit kneels beside him and wipes his face with a cloth. Here, the actor playing Mr Dorrit seems to notice his daughter for the first time. 'Amy, I tell you, if you could see me as your mother saw me, you would not believe it to be the creature you have only looked at through the bars of this cage.'

Little Dorrit tries to take his hand, but he resists it.

'Unless my face, when I am dead, subsides into the long departed look – they say such things happen, I don't know – my children will never have seen me.'

'Father, don't say so much. Please, father.'

The man's eyes wander, and his face seems to lose some of its expression, as the camera moves now towards him.

'If you could be persuaded to smarten yourself up a little, Amy.'

'Yes, yes, father. But it can't be. It can't be. Don't talk so. That's all over.'

'Cut.'

Spenser Spender was not quite sure about the dialogue at this point. He knew that Rowan Phillips had taken it almost directly from the novel but as a result it sounded somewhat artificial, contrived. But then, on the other hand, it had a certain ring, a certain gravity, to it. If the images could match the grandiloquence of the words, then it might work. The prison sequences would need to be very powerful indeed, though. He would need more time here.

Still, the father had seemed too morose, not crazy enough, in the first take. He took the actor to one side, and mimicked the expressions he wanted from him in a kind of dumb-show. Little Dorrit sat on a small canvas chair while a young man applied more cream and powder to her face. Again, the lights were switched on. There was no sound, and the voices of the two protagonists sounded faint and small in the space of the vast prison landing. A bird could be heard rustling in the roof, but the microphone would not record it.

'What does it matter whether I die here or not—'

At this moment, there was a loud crack, as though a plank had snapped in two, and one of the smaller arc-lights fell from the metal stairs to which it had been attached. It fell upon the ground with a thud, and its cable snapped and rose into the air, lashing one of the technicians across the face. He fell down against the wall, in much the same position as Mr Dorrit had assumed but with more conviction. The cut across his face was jagged and bleeding, and he was surrounded at once by other members of the crew. They helped him up and took him outside while Spenser Spender looked on in astonishment. The arc-light lay shattered upon the floor.

'I knew there was a jinx on this place,' Little Dorrit murmured to her father, who made no attempt to move, 'I knew it as soon as I saw it. I hate it here.' Spenser Spender called a halt to shooting that day.

The incident quickly became a subject of gossip within the prison itself. The inmates treated it with scarcely-concealed satisfaction and, by the time the story reached Little Arthur, it had grown larger and more colourful in the telling. It seemed that a part of the wall had fallen down – that wing was known to have been built on shaky foundations – and it had dragged all the lights with it. The electricity had gone right across the landings and up the bars of the cells, like a whiplash. Some of them had heard the crash, and heard the actors screaming blue murder; but the governor had hushed it up. It would have been bad publicity.

When Little Arthur heard the details, he danced around his cell, making strange bark-like noises and tapping the bars of his door to a staccato beat. 'It's coming to a head—' he shouted out loud – 'It's coming to a head. There will be electricity. I told them so.' Pally had also heard about the 'disaster' in the old wing. He wiped his mouth, as though trying to remove it from his face, and stared at the wall while the other two inmates in his cell discussed it. He could not bring himself to say anything, and they would laugh at him in any case. But he knew about it, all right, he knew.

twenty-two

After the first flush of exhilaration, when Rowan had finished the script of *Little Dorrit* and Spenser Spender had said that, actually, Rowan, this is very good, just what we need, Rowan had felt that somehow he had risen out of Cambridge. He was perpetually dissatisfied and ill at ease, continually wanting to escape from whatever bonds or responsibilities that held him. Now that he had achieved something in what he described to his colleagues as the movies he felt estranged from Cambridge. The literary and academic worlds, which he had pursued so assiduously and joined with such enthusiasm, now seemed to him to be small and parochial.

'Cambridge,' he would say to one or two of his college associates, 'is a university looking for the knowledge to sustain itself – a scholastic vampire.' 'Looking towards the future here,' he would say to his more favoured pupils, 'is like trying to read a road map at midnight.' It was in this mood that he asked Tim down for the weekend; it was an act of defiance and self-assertion.

Tim and Rowan had continued their friendship in much the same way as it had first been established: their first encounter had been, for Tim, so traumatic and, for Rowan, so unexpected and so much to be hoped for, that it had been frozen in time; it had become an emblem of the way things were, and had to be. Any deviation from the set pattern might run the risk of undermining it completely. But Rowan knew that matters could not continue in this way for ever: he wanted to test Tim in some new situation, to see if the bonds of their relationship – as he now thought of it – could stand the strain. And his emotional life was the one area where he could experiment, he knew, without doing any serious damage to himself.

'Tim,' he mentioned as if on a sudden inspiration one

evening, 'how would you feel about coming down, I mean coming up, to Cambridge one weekend?'

'I wouldn't say no, Rowan. But I see Aud on Sundays. I always see her on Sundays.'

'I'm sure that Audrey can manage, Tim.'

'I don't know about that. You said yourself she needs constant attention, like.'

'She can do without you for one afternoon. Be reasonable.'

'Give us a day or two to think about it, Rowan. I don't want Aud getting all upset.'

'She could hardly get more upset than she is already, could she?'

'Don't talk like that, Rowan.' Tim had begun to assert himself more in conversation with Rowan, perhaps in order to compensate for his passivity in their brief sexual encounters. 'You know Aud's in a bad state. Me and her go back a long way.'

'Don't we all,' muttered Rowan. But he knew he would get his way.

Rowan met Tim at Cambridge station and, in that uncharacteristic environment, they looked upon each other in a new light. Tim didn't look quite so handsome as he used to, Rowan thought. Rowan seemed nervous, edgy, difficult to talk to, Tim thought.

Tim had expected Cambridge to be like the universities he had seen on television – he expected to see thousands upon thousands of students, all wearing gowns, clutching mascots, and roaring with laughter. He imagined the buildings would resemble St Trinian's, but on a grander scale. He was a little disappointed by the time they had reached Rowan's own rooms. The whole place seemed dead, empty, no life to it.

Rowan ushered him in hurriedly, and slammed the door.

'So this is where I spend most of my time you see, Tim. Very different from London, isn't it?'

Tim was not as impressed by the surroundings as Rowan had hoped, and expected, him to be. He merely looked bemused. 'Yes, it's very nice, Rowan, sort of home from home really.'

'That's what it's meant to be, Tim. Exactly. A home from

126

home.' Rowan was energetically arranging and re-arranging things; he was like a budgerigar whose cage has been invaded by a prying finger.

'How do you manage without a TV then?'

'Oh I hardly need it, Tim. I do have my work, you know.'

'But you've got a TV in London.'

Rowan had in fact been planning to hire a television set, and hide it in his cupboard during tutorials; he had been wanting one for months. 'That's different, Tim. I don't really work in London. It's my holiday camp.'

'Oh I see.'

Tim was puzzled; Rowan had insisted that he came down to see him, but now he was behaving as if he didn't want him here. He felt awkward, out of place.

Rowan made tea, for want of anything better to do. They sat facing each other, Tim on the couch and Rowan in an armchair, balancing their cups upon their knees, remarking upon the furnishings in the room and how different they were from those in the London flat, and how quiet it was here compared to London, when there was a tentative knock on the door. Rowan jumped up and spilt his tea; he looked wildly at Tim, as though Tim were responsible for whatever dread summons it turned out to be. Tim shifted uncomfortably and gulped his tea, keeping his eyes upon the worn carpet.

He raised them as Rowan opened the door and saw a smooth, reddish face pop around it like a puppet from behind a curtain. It might have been a young face, were it not for the thatch of white and greying hair which stuck out at all angles.

'I'm sorry, Wowan, is this a wotten time?' The voice was curiously flat and high; its owner flinched as Rowan put a hand on his arm – as much to steady himself as anything else.

'No, not at all, Michael. Do come in.'

Michael almost fell into the room, his white hair streaming out behind him. He looked at Tim and then back at Rowan with a bright, perhaps manic, stare; he might have been in some kind of trance.

'I don't think you know Timothy Coleman, Michael. Timothy, this is Michael Dickey, one of my colleagues.'

'How nice to meet you, Mr Coleman.' Michael scratched his leg for no apparent reason. 'How vewy vewy nice.'

'Nice meeting you, too.'

Rowan was pretending to himself that nothing whatever was happening. He was in a state of defensive shock. His two worlds had collided – an event he had in a sense wished upon himself but which now, at the moment of impact, seemed to threaten him in deep and unexpected ways. He poured a cup of tea for the visitor.

'Are you weally sure I'm not intewwupting anything, Wowan?' Michael leaned forward in his chair, as if he were speaking to a very deaf person and needed to make himself absolutely clear. He scratched himself again.

'No, not at all, Michael. Not in the least.'

'It was weally about college business, an awful bore for you on your day off as it were.' Michael gave another wide-eyed glance at Tim, who looked down again at the carpet.

'No. That's fine. That's fine.'

'Well,' he hunched himself forward, 'it's about this libwawy committee. The secwetary has turned everything upside down and we can't find any twace of 77 to 78. Are you with me?' Rowan nodded: he would do anything to prevent the conversation touching on personal matters, such as his friends in London who came to visit him here. 'The Master doesn't want to know of course. If he had his way, we would never order a book again. He calls it a wecession. More like a wetweat, it seems to me.'

Rowan stared hard at Michael, almost physically preventing himself from directing even an odd glance at Timothy. Michael, implicitly acknowledging the situation, stared back at Rowan. Everyone in the college 'knew' that Rowan was homosexual, but such mild eccentricities were of no account in a place where the subject of sex itself was never raised. As far as Michael was concerned, Tim was invisible.

Tim slowly comprehended this fact, and an angry will rose up in him. He got up from the sofa, and stood there for a second until Rowan looked up at him, annoyed. 'Excuse me, Rowan, I'm just going to stretch me legs. I'll see you later, all right?' He walked to the door without saying anything to

Dickey; the two men watched the door close, looked quickly at each other, and resumed their conversation.

He had been walking for about an hour, along the bank of a narrow river; he went past two or three colleges, and then wandered across a public park. Young couples walked slowly here, with their children shouting and screaming amongst the trees: Tim thought of Audrey, and what might have been their life together. An old man was playing tennis with a young girl, a middle-aged woman was asleep upon a bench. The emptiness of the afternoon filled Tim with a sorrow which he had not experienced before: perhaps all his days had been like this, white and expansive like clouds moving over an empty sky. He followed the river-bank until he came to a small metal bridge. He walked over the bridge and, on the other side of the bank, saw that he was on the fringes of a council-house estate. He had come from such places, played in them when a child and, in all probability, would be returning to them. His life was bounded by the dull red bricks and the tiny gardens.

Rowan Phillips knew nothing of such things – which was why Tim both needed him and was apprehensive of him. Rowan's world was one of comfort. There was something fascinating about him – his nervous talk, the way he never checked his change in pubs, his queerness. Tim needed someone like that, to lead him to some higher ground and show him the world. He decided that he would apologise to Rowan for his behaviour.

When Tim returned, still red-faced from running all the way back, Rowan was alone. 'What made you walk out like that, Tim? It wasn't very polite, was it? It wasn't very polite to Michael.'

'I'm sorry, Rowan. I just wanted to stretch me legs.'

'Oh, I see. I suppose that explains it.'

Rowan was angry, although he could not have said why and he could no more have expressed his anger than a dumb man speak syllables. But Tim sensed it, and felt helpless within it. He knew only one way to make amends. He lay down on the sofa, with one leg stretched out on to the floor, giving every sign that he was willing to let Rowan suck or blow.

Any human relationship is poised on so delicate an equilibrium that it can be disturbed and destroyed in a moment. Rowan was nonplussed by Tim's apparent readiness and even eagerness to have sex. They were about to become equal partners in what had been Rowan's private pursuit. Tim had been an emblem of what for Rowan had always been unattainable, romantic even: that vast and chaotic urban life which had before existed for him only in books. Now, however, the unattainable was becoming all too attainable.

He knelt beside Tim but, even before he began the customary preliminaries, he knew that it was not going to work. He stood up and brushed some fluff off his trousers, 'I'm sorry, Tim, but I don't really feel like it now. Maybe later on.'

Tim looked surprised and slightly hurt: a present he had offered had been unceremoniously handed back to him, without even the wrapping removed. His original irritation returned. 'Please yourself, Rowan. It don't bother me.'

And so they struggled through the afternoon, with attempts at casual conversation, with a walk through the colleges which seemed to Tim like a large open-air prison, with a short sleep that left them both edgy and dissatisfied. Both of them knew that something had gone wrong, and each of them blamed the other for it.

As soon as he could, Rowan took refuge in his cupboard and emerged with the sherry bottle. They drank in silence, the sweet taste making Tim feel sick and giddy. Rowan contemplated the situation.

'So where shall we go and eat, Timothy?' He had been thinking of taking him into Hall, but that was quite out of the question now. He had to protect his interests. 'Where shall we go, old boy, as the English say?'

'I don't know really. Whatever you want. Was that sherry off, then?'

'Yes, it was off, old boy. I bought it specially for you.' Tim knew that Rowan was making fun of him in some way, but could not decide how or why. Rowan, whenever he was ill at ease, became impatient. 'There is this delightful little Indian restaurant just across the street. Will that be suitable for you, Timothy, my man?'

'Whatever you say, Rowan.'

They left the room quickly, seeking the anonymity of the restaurant.

Tim in fact disliked Indian food, but he didn't want to cause any more fuss. With each spoonful of chicken curry and vegetable biryani that he swallowed, he took a large gulp of white wine. The food on his plate seemed to congeal into soggy balls of rice and grey, straggling and quite unrecognisable vegetables. After a while, he simply ignored his food, and drank. As he drank, he became more talkative, the resentments of the day spilling over the brim.

'Have you ever tried it with girls then, Rowan?'

'Once or twice, I suppose.' As Rowan lied, he looked around at the other tables to make sure that no one was listening to their conversation.

'And did you enjoy it, then?'

'I guess so, yes. You've asked me all this before, Tim. It gets very boring for me.'

'So why do you fancy me then?'

'I don't know, Tim. I really don't know. Do we have to talk about it in public?'

'I'm just interested, squire, that's all.'

'Well then, Timothy, you answer me a question for once. Why do you let me do it?'

Tim poured himself another glass of wine, and looked down at his plate of cold curry. 'Well, I like you, don't I? You're my mate. Of course it's different with Audrey. I love Audrey. I did things with Audrey you wouldn't believe, Rowan. Honest. She was great in bed – before she went daft, like.'

When Tim talks like this, Rowan thought, he becomes terribly dull.

'She's a great girl, Audrey. She's got great tits, but I really respected her. Do you know what I mean?'

'I suppose so.'

'But don't get me wrong, Rowan. I really like you, you old poof.'

An Indian waiter seemed to have appeared from nowhere, like a devil in a pantomime, and was already at Tim's shoulder as he spoke. Rowan blanched with embarrassment,

131

as the waiter slowly cleared away their plates. To think this was happening to him, in his own Cambridge. He could never come into this restaurant again.

When the waiter retreated, Rowan's embarrassment had already turned to anger. Had he spent so much time and effort on this boy, only to be labelled a 'poof'?

'And I suppose you had the best of relationships with Audrey, too. Is that right? Is that why she went mad?'

'That's got nothing to do with it.'

'Of course it has. Nothing is one-sided. You are just as responsible as anyone else for what's happening to her.' In his fury, he began to sympathise with Audrey: he became Audrey for the time being. 'It's no good reading me lectures about the joys of sex, when you couldn't even keep up a decent relationship with the one girl who you say you love.'

Tim stared at Rowan; he was biting his upper lip, and banging his knees together beneath the table. He was at war with himself. He wanted to hit Rowan. And yet he needed him. He needed someone.

'You can be very cruel, you know. Rowan. Bitchy, like.'

Rowan looked over at the other tables; he had raised his voice, and now felt somewhat abashed. 'I'm only telling the truth, Tim. You called me an old poof, remember.'

Their argument subsided. Tim, drunk now and frightened of alienating Rowan, was trying to be affectionate. He retold jokes he had heard at work. Rowan laughed at them, while all the time contemplating the mistake he had made: it was foolish of him to expect that he and Tim could strike up any kind of solid relationship. They could hardly be friends, let alone lovers. But he didn't blame himself. Such things happened. It was the way of the world. The only thing that concerned him now was to extricate himself from the situation without risking a 'scene', as he thought of it, from Tim.

After they had left the restaurant, Tim was sick against the walls of the college. Rowan watched him dispassionately, made no move towards him. They went back to Rowan's rooms, went to bed, and fell asleep almost at once. Rowan took the lead by pretending to do so, muttering and turning over – Tim followed, naturally and drunkenly, into a real oblivion.

On the train back to London the next morning – Tim had to see Audrey that afternoon since he thought that, if he broke the routine once, it would break down for ever – Rowan was cheerful and talkative. Tim felt reassured: he had managed to smooth things over. Rowan felt a slight pang of regret about leaving Tim: he was after all a good-looking boy with a normally pleasant nature. But it had to be done. Tim, entering the spirit of Rowan's cheerfulness, was making plans for him to meet his parents, just as a friend like. Rowan smiled and nodded. He would love to meet Tim's parents, he really would; and then he went on to describe the accident on the film set at the prison. I suppose it was fate, he was saying, because disasters and accidents don't happen by chance. They teach us something, don't they, Tim? Tim nodded, and looked out at the streets and hoardings as the train entered London, slowing down as though it were entering a grey swamp.

They shook hands at Liverpool Street Station. Rowan had told Tim that he was going to meet Spenser Spender, but in fact he was going straight back to Cambridge. Mission complete. He smiled again at Tim, who suddenly and clumsily reached towards Rowan and kissed him on the cheek. Rowan stepped back, discomforted, and they both again said goodbye. As he watched Tim walking towards the underground, Rowan was sure that he would never see him again. But in this, as in so many things, he was to prove mistaken.

twenty-three

Andrew and Laetitia had another fight, over nothing in particular; these arguments were becoming so regular now that they resembled one long feud, with various and intermittent battles to break up the monotony of cool enmity. Laetitia was daily expecting a letter from Spenser Spender's solicitors: and she knew that, when it arrived, her impossible situation would at last become official. It would then require treatment, and cure.

Until that time came, she simply floated in her lake of lethargy and depression, spending what little energy she had in keeping herself from disappearing under its waters. She had been to see her doctor; she had almost gladly revealed the indignity of her venereal disease, displaying her pointless and decaying life, as she thought, to someone who might shock her into action. She was hoping, at the least, for a lecture on the dangers of promiscuity. Instead, the doctor simply gave her some pills, and told her not to have sex for three weeks. It seemed to Laetitia that the whole world was bland now, and unfeeling.

It was after her fight with Andrew that Laetitia went on one of her long, aimless walks through the streets of London. She had now adopted the habit of scrutinising each face she passed for signs of an unhappiness similar to her own. These days, it seemed to her that the people she saw might be creatures from some dream of the past – the workman with his flat cap, grinning to himself; the old woman, curved over like a plant that had forgotten the sun, shuffling across an ancient courtyard; the young boy, pale, ragged, scuttling along the streets as if the offices and houses themselves frightened him, threatened to beat him. She saw all of these people on her journey, flashing across her vision so rapidly that they became types: they represented this city, they existed in no other place. The strength and the darkness of London had compressed itself into these tiny, wandering forms. She could have drowned in it, she thought, like the old woman with the prams. When had she seen her last? It was winter: she and Spenser were walking somewhere, arm in arm. Had the old woman survived the cold?

She joined a queue for the bus back to Shepherd's Bush. Everyone around her looked shabby and dirty – the whole city was undergoing some fundamental deterioration which marked its inhabitants like the evidence of some ugly disease. Such was her private distress that she could normally think of such matters resignedly, almost cheerfully: any corroboration of her condition was better than none. She did not want to be alone. But, on this afternoon, her depression was such that the evidence of decay elsewhere simply pulled her down even further into the depths of the emptiness which she sensed within herself. Her head ached; it felt constricted, crushed.

She sat on top of the bus, behind a couple with a small child. The man was wearing a faded leather jacket, and his jeans and shoes were scuffed, old. His wife was in a shapeless knitted sweater and an old skirt, balancing two shopping bags on her knees. Their little girl, no more than five or six, had dark rings under her eyes; she was sitting in front of her parents, and at any sign of conversation between them she would perk up, and turn round, her eyes shining. But, since there seemed to be very little her parents could find to say to each other, the little girl would ask them questions, to spur them into life. 'Mummy,' she was saying, 'are there always flowers after winter?' Her parents hardly noticed her, and made no attempt to reply. They were trapped in some bewildered world of privation and disappointment. 'Mummy,' she asked again, 'are there always flowers after winter?' There was still no answer. The child put her head down against the seat, and stared at the yellow ceiling of the bus.

Laetitia was watching this small scene intently, as if somehow she were involved in the action. The child's question, and the subsequent silence from her parents, for some reason brought tears to her eyes. She sat on the bus, her

135

tears a witness to her own misery, if anyone had noticed – but no one had.

She left the bus at Shepherd's Bush, and pushed her way through the crowds of men and women returning from their work. She went back to the flat like a sleep walker who has no control or interest in her destination; the flat was empty. She knew it would be. Andrew had gone out on a job – working as an extra on some night shooting for an American film – and he would not be back until the morning. She lay down on the narrow bed and considered her life – that it had all come down to this point, that everything she had done or thought had only resulted in this tear-stained woman lying in a small flat. What could you do with such a creature? You could only pity it, you could not help it. You might try to put it out of its misery.

She got up quickly from the bed and went over to the drawer where Andrew kept his pills – valium, librium, mandrax. She poured them into a heap upon the table, multi-coloured, the magic mountain, she thought. She started swallowing them one by one, and then in handfuls, but her throat was too dry. She went over to the sink and poured a cup of water. She swallowed the rest. Then she switched on the television. She watched a cookery class – the food seemed too bright, not like real food. She ought to write a note to Spenser. The cookery was over; now there was a programme about a hotel. They were all laughing at something. She must write and tell him that she loved him. She started fumbling in the desk for a pen, but, by then, it was too late.

Andrew returned to the flat much earlier than he had planned; it had started to rain, and the shooting for that night had been called off. He hated going back to Shepherd's Bush, but he had arranged nothing else for the night. At least he could change, make a few calls. The thought of spending the evening with Letty was just too boring. He was getting annoyed with her these days: she wasn't turning out to be as much fun as he had hoped, and sometimes she even got ratty with his friends, which was unforgivable. There would have to be a parting of the ways soon, old girl – he rehearsed the lines in his mind as he opened the front door of the flat.

Some large doll had been deposited upon the floor, or a

mannequin had broken and fallen over. An awful joke by someone. It took him a few seconds to realise that the thing lying there was Laetitia. He turned on the light and, in the sudden glare, her face looked blurred and distorted. He skirted around the body, peering at it without actually getting too close, and then telephoned for an ambulance. He went and sat in the bathroom. He could not bear to be in the same room with it.

He came to life again when they entered the flat, the smile hovering over his face until he realised that it was inappropriate.

'I haven't moved her, officer. I believe that is the right thing.'

They bent over her, opening her mouth, feeling her pulse. 'Do you have any idea what caused this, sir?'

'No, I'm afraid I don't. I just got home and there it, there she, was.'

One of the ambulancemen went over to the desk and picked up the empty bottles of pills. Andrew had not noticed them there; he felt hot and uncomfortable now – he wanted a bath. An oxygen mask had been placed over Laetitia's mouth and she was moved on to a stretcher,

'Is she alive?' Andrew thought the question sounded right.

'Just about. Were you close to her?'

'No. She was just a friend really.'

'Can you give me her name?'

'Spender, Mrs Spender.'

'Well, we're taking Mrs Spender to Hammersmith Hospital. Someone will be in touch with you shortly.'

'What about?'

The ambulanceman looked surprised. 'To tell you how she is. Get the names of next of kin and so on. Are you with me?' He assumed Andrew was in shock, but he was merely alarmed.

'Oh. Yes, yes, I am.'

After they had gone, the siren sounding through the night, Andrew took out a cigarette, sat on the edge of the bed, and tried to calm himself. He would have to 'phone Spenser Spender – that would be a bore, but it was necessary. It was best to get these things over with as quickly as possible. He hoped she didn't die; he could not bear the thought of a coroner's inquest, and being questioned about all those pills. He wanted to make a quick exit out of what might prove to be a difficult situation.

Spenser Spender was sitting at home, staring out of the window as the darkness settled down. He was contemplating the fiasco in the prison. The technician had been taken to the hospital, to have a few stitches in his face. It had been an inauspicious start; he was relying upon the prison sequences to give the film its special identity, and the atmosphere had been soured by a stupid accident. He might never get it right now. The 'phone rang, and he knew it was going to be more bad news. He went to it unwillingly.

'Hello? Is that Spenser?'

'Yes.'

'Oh hi. This is Andrew, you know, Letty's friend.'

'Yes. I know. What's happened?' He knew that something, or someone, had injured Laetitia, and his stomach turned over.

'Letty has swallowed some pills. It was nothing to do with me, I can tell you that. Well anyway, they've taken her to hospital now. I think she's going to be all right.'

'What hospital?'

'Hammersmith, you know, by the—'

Spenser put the 'phone down and sat in the darkness; he could not take in what he had just heard. He noticed that a kind of light filtered through the closed door; even though it was evening now, it seemed to be brighter outside than it was in the room. Perhaps he could use that effect in the film. But he was already on his feet. Without thinking, he switched on a lamp, and left the flat.

The hospital itself, he realised as he drew up in a taxi, he knew only from the outside. It was next to the prison and had, in his imagination, always been part of it. The whole of his life seemed to merge at this one point, this small area of the world – and was it simply fortuitous that he had also been born here? Inside, the hospital had the faded, dilapidated air of institutionalised concern; there was a small florist's shop in one corner of the entrance-hall, and a confectioner's in

138

another. Small groups of people sat around, with bags and packages, watching one another. It was like a railway station in which all the trains were postponed, or derailed.

Spenser went up to the reception desk and enquired where he might find Mrs Spender – she had been brought in a little while ago, after swallowing some pills. The words themselves sounded so leaden, so heavily appropriate to the small facts of the matter – he was taking part, automatically, in a ritual over which he no longer had any control. Telephone calls were made. The receptionist suggested that he take a seat, and someone would be down directly. He dragged a vacant chair to one side of the large room, and waited. Somewhere, in this place, she was lying upon a bed. She had not left him – really, he had abandoned her. She had tried to kill herself because he had not loved her enough.

'Mr Spender?'

'Yes?' He got up from the chair too hastily, and it fell to the floor with a loud crash.

'Are you the person who telephoned for an ambulance?'

'No. That was someone else. Someone my wife knew. How is she? How is my wife?'

'She is out of danger now and resting comfortably.'

'Can I see her?'

'I'm afraid not, no. She'll be asleep until tomorrow morning.' It was only now that Spenser realised that he was talking to a young man, almost a boy, he thought. He did not know what else to say, or ask.

'Will you tell her I came as soon as I knew?'

'Yes, we'll tell her.'

'Right.' He hesitated. 'I'll be here tomorrow morning. That's right, isn't it?'

'Yes, that's right.'

Spenser walked out of the hospital and leant against the nearest bus stop. What had Letty said? Those who are the saddest are capable of the greatest happiness. He did not really know why she had tried to kill herself, what her feelings were. Perhaps this was now the opportunity for the two of them to come closer together, to break down the barriers which they had instinctively built between each other. He saw Letty walking towards him, with the light behind her,

139

as in a film. A bus came, and he got on it. Two adults, redeemed by the power of love, a new life. After a few minutes, he realised that he was travelling in the wrong direction. He got off the bus in panic, and tried to find his way home.

Spenser woke early the next morning – it was lucky, he thought, the prison being so close to the hospital, when he remembered why it was that he was going there. His own forgetfulness – or was it lack of feeling? – made him groan into the pillow. He tried to create within himself a new resolve: Lettuce and he, no, Laetitia and he would make a new start. He would tell her at the hospital.

She looked pale, drained, as though the drip in her arm were actually taking the energy out of her body and distributing it to the walls and floors of the hospital itself. Her breathing seemed shallow, but she turned towards Spenser when he tentatively touched her shoulder.

'It's you.'

'Yes, Letty, it's me.'

He sat next to her, and she seemed to drift into sleep. But her eyes, averted from Spenser, were open.

'How are you?' she said.

'I'm fine. The film's going well, apart from a few small hiccups. We're just next door you know, back in the old prison. You remember I was trying to get it for—' She had turned her face away from him again. 'Oh I'm sorry, Letty, you don't want to hear about all this what with you—'

'Yes, I do. Go on.'

'No, Letty. I want to think about you. Will you come on home now, after this?'

'I suppose so.'

There was a silence between them.

'How are you feeling, Letty?'

'I don't know. Sometimes I just feel dead inside.'

'You know you shouldn't say things like that.' She looked at him almost with pity. He really didn't know what else to say. 'I want you back, Letty, you know. I can't live without you.'

'I want to come back, too.'

'And we'll be cosy together, right?'

'Right.'

'I'll look after you like you were my little baby. Would you like that, little lettuce leaf?'

'Yes.'

She smiled and closed her eyes, saying nothing else. Spenser guessed that she had drifted into sleep and, after a few minutes, he went quietly away. He left a message on the table by her bed: 'I'll be back tonight. Pops.' When she heard him getting up and walking away, Laetitia opened her eyes and watched him as he moved, self-consciously, down the narrow corridor between the beds. Despite his blindness to her, she loved him; or, at least, she needed him – she was no longer sure of the distinction. She knew that there was no other place for her to go; no other place, but the old world with Spenser, was open to her. She curled up and pulled the sheets closely round her body, like a child.

Spenser walked out into the street, and towards the prison, joyful. Everything was back where it should be. He could continue the filming with a clear conscience, all conflicts resolved. He did not think for long about Laetitia's attempted suicide, and he knew that he would never mention it to her again. They would wipe out the past.

It was only when he was within a few feet of the prison gates that he noticed the crew; they were huddled in small groups, conferring about something. Some of them were pretending not to see him, and looked abashed.

twenty-four

When Tim visited Audrey the following Sunday, a week after his visit to Cambridge, Audrey announced to him – triumphantly almost – that she had been sacked from her job at the telephone exchange. 'I don't care,' she said, 'they can stuff it, they can.' She glared at him, as if she thought for a moment that he might have been responsible for her dismissal. 'I told you, didn't I, about the clever ones. Now they've gone and told the Post Office to give me the push.' She lit a cigarette – this was a new habit, but Tim was too surprised by what she had told him to pay much attention to it – and in her nervous excitement she had dropped the lighted match from her fingers as she walked about the room. Tim hastened to stamp it out with his foot, but the smell of burning wafted up from the carpet.

'I suppose,' Audrey was saying, 'they think they can get away with it. Well, I'll show them, I will.' She put her hand up to her forehead, in order to stop the shaking which infected her whole body. 'They can't break me down. They don't know what they're dealing with in Audrey Skelton.'

Tim was by now accustomed to Audrey's suddenly aggressive moods and had come to accept them as another sign of what was happening all around him. He felt uncertain and ill at ease, and in some way he was beginning to appreciate, if not wholly understand, Audrey's bizarre behaviour. She was right to get upset, the way the world was going. The fact that he had been to visit Rowan Phillips on his usual night, and that Rowan had not been there, had not even left a message, reinforced his feelings of rejection and uncertainty. He could not understand why Rowan had not been in touch – they seemed to have got on so well in Cambridge – and, like Audrey, he began to feel that it was a question of 'them' and 'us'. Rowan lived to rules which were not Tim's; Tim felt that

142

he was at the losing end of whatever double standards were in use. But he was baffled; he needed guidance, and he would take it from wherever it came.

'So what are you going to do, Aud?' He was following her around the room with an ashtray.

'Oh act your age, Timothy Coleman. You with your Mr God Almighty author, what's-his-name.'

'What do you mean?'

'Oh don't act daft, Tim. You come on all sweet and innocent. You should be ashamed of yourself, you really should. They've taken you for a ride and you know it.'

This confirmed Tim's suspicion that Audrey had somehow found out about him and Rowan. It was to be expected.

'I'm sorry, Audrey.' His voice went too high, and he coughed. 'I didn't know about him. He was all friendly like, to begin with.'

'Well then, you're a bigger fool than I took you for.'

'Anyway, that's all stopped now.'

'And wasn't I right all along?'

'Yeah, you were right all right. You don't know where you are with writers and such like. They're all over you one minute and forgotten about you the next.'

If Audrey had been listening properly to Tim, she would have recognised how confused, how unhappy, he was. But she took his confession as a further confirmation of her own grievances. It could not be said, in fact, that Tim's perception of his own position was markedly different from Audrey's. He felt humiliated and betrayed – but he could not see any way of changing himself or the world. In this situation, all he could do was attach himself to Audrey and her forceful presentation of her wrongs. The smell of burning was still lingering in the air.

They both sat in silence, savouring their loneliness, unable to find words to cover their position.

'So what are you going to do about a job, Aud?'

'Well, there are plenty out of work aren't there?' She lit another cigarette. 'I don't know. What does anybody do?'

'Get in the dole queue, I suppose.'

Audrey now was more composed; her immediate personal

predicament had brought her back to herself. 'God, I hate the lot of them. I hate the fucking post office, the fucking government. They can all burn in Hell.' She stubbed out the cigarette in the ashtray which Tim now held out to her.

twenty-five

Little Arthur sits in his cell and wiggles his toes. It is the recreation period, and the shouts and cries of the prison reverberate around him. But Little Arthur hears these sounds only subliminally, as a horseman might hear the sound of birds on his travels; Arthur uses his time to continue with the plan, moving through it, stage by stage, day by day, not wishing to anticipate the next point, and the next. There is virtue in slowness, in inevitability. He understands this ever since the reverend preacher, the most high man, visited him.

The reverend had swept into Arthur's cell one evening, just as twilight fell, and told Arthur that he would pray for his immortal soul and did he need anything? Little Arthur had snorted, and done a somersault on his hard prison bed – as if to say, look at me now and here I am. Do I look as if I need anything from one as tall as you? And then the reverend preacher – dressed all in black, as black as soot, as black as an uncleaned machine, thought Arthur – had opened his little black book and read a passage. 'A favourite of mine, Feather, and a constant source of joy. Blessed are the poor, for theirs is the kingdom of God etcetera etcetera. Now let me see. Blessed are those that weep now, for they shall laugh. Blessed are the lowly for they shall see God.'

'Stop right there, reverend. I like that part. Read that again.'

'Blessed are the lowly for they shall be exalted, see God, I mean.'

'I knew it! I knew it all along!' He rose from his bunk, and hauled himself up so that he could see through the barred window of his cell, forgetting the presence of the reverend in his excitement. 'I knew it was there all along!'

After that, Little Arthur asked for regular visits from the

prison chaplain. He would question him carefully, and write down his answers in a small note-book.

'And how will the world end?'

'Certain authorities, Feather, have declared that it will end in fire. But I believe in keeping an open mind on such matters. It is a morbid subject, Feather, a morbid subject.'

'I wouldn't say so, reverend. There's a lot of meaning in it, if you ask me, packed full of meaning.'

'What it means, Feather, is that sinners will be purified on the last day, the evil made good, the good made bright, as if by fire.'

'Yes, I like that. I like the sound of that.'

'We are all sinners, Feather, even those of us who have not been brought to this place.'

'Oh yes, that's ripe, that is. So when is all this fire going to happen?' Little Arthur pretended to be very interested in the back of his hand, but looked keenly up at the reverend as he waited for his answer.

'In God's time, not ours.'

Such conversations left Little Arthur in a state of great anticipation; it was not until he came to prison that he had had the time to contemplate such things. He had always been too busy before. Now he spent hours just sitting and brooding. Here, also, no one paid him much attention. He could watch and watch, without feeling the eyes upon him. The result of his watching was to confirm what he had always believed about them and their world. Their world – the strangeness of it, the ritual, the pointlessness – was just as he thought.

He had made one friend within the prison, Pally, to whom he could impart his thoughts. Pally had been moved to the segregated section as well – he had adopted the habit of banging his head against the walls of his cell until it became wounded and bloody, and was as a result transferred to this better-supervised area. Little Arthur would meet Pally in the meal-queue, and whisper his new knowledge to him. 'I've heard all about it from the reverend,' he said one morning. 'It will all end in fire. What do you think about that then?' He pinched Pally excitedly; Pally smiled and nodded his head. 'We'll bring it all down round their heads, won't we, Pally?'

He aimed playful jabs at Pally's stomach, which Pally would – with equal good humour – ward off with his hands. 'We'll show them, won't we, Pally, show them up for what they are!' Pally smiled.

It was on the following morning that Little Arthur saw the film crew arrive, with their lights and their cables. He was reminded of Fun City and all the electricity which he had held there. And the old resentment came up in him again, at the thought of the power of which he had been deprived. Perhaps the men in the green vans had taken it – perhaps they had stolen the power of Fun City.

And then he saw her – a small, pale girl, thin, in some kind of old grey dress. She was surrounded by men who kept on putting marks on her face, laughing at her. Could it really be her, his little love, all over again? He waved and shouted at her from behind the bars of his window. He could have sworn that she looked up at him. Yes, it was his little angel. She had got up from the park and ran away when all those people came. And now, yes, she was being taken inside the prison with all the lights and wires.

He sat down upon his bunk, and took out his notebook. He knew that they had lied to him all along, that she was still alive. When he had been put in the dock, your honour, when people had talked about him, my lord, stared at him, pointed at him, smiled at him, he had wondered where she was. In his police cell he had drawn pictures of her on scraps of paper – starting with her neck, he would draw lines upwards until they became her hair, and also flames.

But now she was trapped with them. They had brought her here to mock him, to show him that he was powerless to help her. They would bind her hair with wires, and the lights would burn upon her neck. She had looked up at him just then, pleading for help. He had to rescue her. The reverend preacher had said it out loud, the lowly shall be exalted. He had admitted it.

He rocks up and down upon his bed, as he did when he was young. He looks at his drawings of the little angel and he kisses them. The lowly shall be exalted. He opens a clean page of his notebook and writes a letter to his love:

Dearest Love, If they trap you with their lights and their machines remember that the heart of you is still yourself. They tell you to do this and do that and they do that to me here but you are not yourself in it are you? I will come for you and as the reverend says the lowly shall be exalted. I think of you so that you may think of me, in the heart of things.

As he writes the letter, he understands what to do. He knows all about electricity, and he knows it will obey him. He is thinking of this, and laughing, when the arc-light falls from its mounting, and the cable lashes across Spenser Spender's crowded film set.

twenty-six

Spenser Spender guessed what had happened as soon as he saw the crew in front of the prison. They had formed a group identity. Their faces had taken on the stubborn anonymity which, like a particular style of portraiture, is immediately recognisable both in period and in meaning.

'Can I speak to you, Mr Spender?' One of the men, who usually judged the level of sound on the set, had stepped forward. He had screwed up his eyes, as though he was looking at Spenser from a distance, and he kept his arms stiffly by his sides.

'Has there been some kind of trouble, Frank?'

'The trouble, as you put it, Mr Spender, is quite obvious. Our brother, Mr Bennett, has suffered severe facial injuries as a result of—'

'You mean the one who cut his cheek?'

'Mr Bennett, as I was saying, suffered severe facial injuries while engaged in highly complicated technical work in an inadequate work environment.'

'The light fell by accident.'

The man hardly seemed to hear Spenser, so great was his concentration, so unshakeable his mien. 'In view of the above-mentioned incident, my members and I have agreed that we cannot work further under these conditions of employment.'

'Oh. I see.'

'We will withdraw our labour until such time as new working procedures are agreed upon by unions and management.'

'You mean you're going to strike?'

The man took a step backwards. 'We are going to withdraw our labour under these unsafe circumstances. My members are not used to working in prisons, nor are they used to

149

having bits of equipment flying about and falling upon their faces.'

'This is all very sudden, Frank.' He looked at the man, who stared down at his shoes.

'We will be following the agreed union and management procedure on this one, Mr Spender. I have informed my union who have given me more than one hundred per cent backing on this, and they have I believe been in official contact with the Film Finance Board.'

Spenser stared at the phalanx of technicians who had now turned their backs upon him and were talking amongst themselves. The actors, too, had formed into a group and looked defiantly around – if he had been thinking of turning to them for comfort, the stares suggested, there was very little that they could offer him. Even the extras had drawn closer together.

'How is he anyway, the one with the cut face?'

The man lowered his voice, in deference to his fallen comrade. 'He is recovering now, thank you very much for asking, Mr Spender. But it came as a severe blow – to himself, naturally, and also to his family. There are no two ways about it, Mr Spender, this so-called set we are using is unsound and a danger to my men.'

The accident had, in fact, shaken Spenser's own confidence in the soundness of the old prison wing. If a small arc-light could fall so quickly, and with such little warning, it was clear that rust and general fatigue permeated the old building. It was clear, also, that he had set the whole electrical system of the prison at risk. That, ironically, had been part of his point – he had wanted to create an atmosphere of menace and decay. But he had never expected that menace to be a real one.

'Surely,' he said, 'we can still work on location elsewhere?'

'I'm afraid, Mr Spender, that this and other matters have now gone to the union sub-committee on demarcation procedures in a strike situation.'

'But what about the set by the river? We can't just leave it there for weeks. The canvas will rot, for a start, and God knows what the vandals will do with it.' Much of the material which Spenser had used for the scenes by the river had been left there – a token guard had been employed, but Spenser had planned to move back to the site very soon. Now the artificial sky would remain suspended indefinitely above the painted streets and buildings. In addition, all of the lights and the electrical equipment had been left in the prison wing. He could not collect them: that area was marked ground. And, besides, there was no one now willing, or able, to help him.

He walked away from the film crew, turned round in order to say something to them, and then thought better of it. He could do nothing, and there was nothing to say. It was as if he were banging his head against thin air and it was still getting bloodied in the process. He relied upon the men who were now putting his work in jeopardy; without them, he was powerless. He was engaged in a battle with people whom he could not afford to defeat. He turned back, and went round the small groups of actors and extras: the film would be delayed for a while, he said, but not for long. He would not let them down.

Sir Frederick Lustlambert, wearing his Film Finance Board hat, was not happy with the situation, not happy at all. Of course he understood Spenser's position, but he had to look at the situation in the round, examine every angle, look at every facet. In a number of telephone calls and letters, Spenser Spender received the distinct impression that he was really to blame for what had occurred. The Film Finance Board understood the union, and the union understood the Film Finance Board. Spenser was, in this situation, the outsider.

Sir Frederick called in Spenser for what he described as a 'chat'. The strike had continued for seven days, and there was no sign of a settlement. The men were demanding a large bonus for working within the prison; the Film Finance Board would not pay such a bonus. Since it would cost a great deal of money to build a set suitable for the prison sequence, the only alternative was to abandon it. Spenser Spender had tried to explain, to both sides, that this would mean altering the entire structure and idea of the film.

Sir Frederick, pointing a chair out to Spenser as though it were an offensive object, asked him if he would like a drink or a cup of coffee perhaps. No, well, he didn't blame him. He was not a coffee man himself. Sir Frederick, perhaps not wishing to allow Spenser to dwell upon this unorthodox confession, launched into his speech. They were both film men, were they not, and they had come across unions before, had they not? Of course he, Sir Frederick, would not stand for their bullying tactics. What the film industry needed, didn't Spenser agree, was a thorough overhaul. Take her apart and put her together again, bang a few heads together, wasn't that the idea? Didn't Mr Spender agree?

'But, Spenser, if I may call you that now, after all, we are old comrades?' He extended his arms as if to embrace Spenser, and Spenser momentarily flinched – 'But, Spenser, I don't think this is the battleground on which we should choose to fight. It is not a black and white situation, is it, Spenser? It is not one-sided. It is not open and shut.'

'Sir Frederick, it was only one arc-light that came off its mounting. It wasn't the end of the world. That kind of thing happens all the time.'

'Yes, Spenser, but the unions are going to turn round to me and say, "Look, Sir Frederick, why use the prison in the first place? That's a no-no, isn't it?" And of course I will defend you. You are my director. When I am wearing my film man's hat, I would be the last person to criticise you on artistic grounds. But say I take off my film hat. Say I take it off—' (Spenser wondered if he should actually say, 'I take if off'. But the pause was majestic only) – 'In my bureaucratic hat I am saying to you, "Think again, Spenser." We need this film, we don't want it ruined.'

'But it will be ruined, Sir Frederick, if we try and change everything at this stage. We've got no money to build an elaborate set. So what am I supposed to do? Shoot a whole different picture without the prison scenes? Would you like *Carry on Dickens?*'

Sir Frederick walked over to the window, his red face and distended nose in clear outline. His back had stiffened and he had wrapped his arms around himself, as if he were in some kind of strait-jacket.

'Spenser, this is a very difficult position for all of us. But we film men have got to be realistic – that is our nature.' He unclasped his arms with difficulty, and went back to the chair behind his desk. 'Imagine now we were in one of the Hollywood studios. There was a strike against the director, holding up production for God know's how long. The director refuses to budge. What would the studio do about that, do you wonder?'

'I don't know. I've never worked in Hollywood, actually.'

'No you haven't, Spenser. And thank God this is London. We are more civilised here. Although I say it myself, we understand artistic matters. But don't forget that all of us, you, even I, are all humble employees of the Film Finance Board.' He turned to the window for a moment, so that Spenser might take in his humble profile. 'We are all, as it were, dispensable. And when the FFB tells us that *Little Dorrit* must be made, then indeed it must be made.' He stood up suddenly. 'Well, Spenser, it's been so nice seeing you again. Why don't we have another chat in a couple of days, when I've had another chance to see the unions about this.' He smiled, and his teeth glinted. He gave his hand across the desk to Spenser, and then quickly took it back as though it might be held in evidence against him.

Spenser left the Film Finance Board with the sense that something had happened. The street seemed the same, the traffic crawled past in its usual manner, but Spenser's relationship to the world had been subtly altered. He had, definitely, been threatened. But so much had been said or implied that he would leave all of it to one side, as one would push away a bill or an uncompleted letter. For the time being, he would think only of Letty, only of her. This afternoon, he had to pick her up from the hospital and take her home. Home is where the heart is. They would start a new life together. At times of crisis in his life, Spenser Spender would instinctively take refuge in platitude; it was his form of whistling in the dark.

She was waiting for him when he came into the ward. She was sitting, dressed, with a small bag at her feet. Her attempt at suicide had exhausted her – she had lost her appetite for movement or drama. She thought to herself, I am a person of little consequence and I will behave like one. Spenser might have discerned traces of this mood upon her countenance, if he had looked for them. But he wanted to see only what he knew.

'Hello, Letty. Time to go home, right?'

'Right.'

Laetitia allowed Spenser to take her bag and, then, her arm as he led her out of the ward. When they walked into the day outside, the light seemed strange to Laetitia after her time inside – too wild, too open. The people were jagged at the edges, their movements sudden and unpredictable. When they arrived home, Spenser made a great fuss of her, putting her to bed, tucking her in, asking her if she would like a little snack or something. No, she just wanted to sleep for a while. Spenser's manner seemed to her forced, self-willed. He had not mentioned her attempt at suicide. The flat was exactly as she had left it – perhaps Spenser was trying to prove that nothing whatever had happened in the intervening months. He had not even mentioned Andrew, or the matter of Laetitia's desertion, and she assumed that he was still too shocked or wounded by those events to discuss them. The fact that he could not even mention Andrew's name was, to her, proof of this. In fact, Spenser Spender had almost forgotten who Andrew was. He was not thinking of him now, and had not done so since he had received the telephone call about Laetitia.

A few minutes later, she was banging on the wall by the bed – he went in to her, and she turned her face away from him, already regretting her helplessness.

'I want some soup and cheese,' she muttered into her pillow.

'Of course, Letty love. I'll get them for you in a jiffy.' He smiled paternally at her. Laetitia hated him for calling her 'Letty love'; she hated herself for demanding soup and cheese when she could perfectly easily prepare them for herself. But now, back in this bed and in this flat, she felt compelled to do so. It was the agony of her ambiguity that had made her thrust her head into the pillow. She saw no way out.

Spenser had not noticed her attitude; he took in her food, and then quietly went out in apparent deference to her weak state. In reality, he wanted time alone to brood. The interview with Sir Frederick only admitted of one result: the world, or at least the bureaucratic world of the Film Finance Board, was about to smother him and *Little Dorrit*. As Sir Frederick had pointed out, he was now only an employee of the Board and, in the eyes of that august cultural institution, only one step higher than a technician. The direction of the film could easily be taken away from him. It was not even as if his own inspiration had failed or disappeared; it was simply that, now, it had come up against the complex but palpable force of other events and other people – for whom his original inspiration was of little importance. *Little Dorrit* had been his vision – he had caught it before it had flown into the vast sphere of unremembered wishes – but, soon, the vision might be all that remained. As he stared out of the window, the old lady with the prams, one before and one behind, walked past down the dead centre of the road. She had, after all, survived the winter. But Spenser did not see her: he was wrapped within his thoughts, blinded by them.

But he wanted to move, to feel free again. He let himself quietly out of the flat, hoping that Laetitia had fallen asleep, and wandered south towards the river and beyond. It was evening now, and the faces of the people he passed seemed curiously expressive. It was as if the twilight and their own tiredness had removed all surface animation, all that was accidental, from their features, and revealed instead their permanent and irretrievable destiny. Spenser's first feeling of despondency had passed, and it was replaced by a settled conviction that his own fate was simply one of millions upon millions tumbling upon each other like a mountain of crystals.

He walked steadily southward over patches of open common and scrub-land. If *Little Dorrit* was altered, or even destroyed and abandoned, it would – it seemed to him on this humid London night – simply be a reminder, a sign, of the common human destiny that he had been foolish enough to think he could avoid. And then he was startled by an irrational happiness that rose up in him. The structures of his problems and difficulties fell away, as the metal supports do from a rocket-launcher. And that sense of harmony and completeness, which had rested with him on Charing Cross

Bridge so many months before, returned now. He had walked for some miles, and when he looked back he saw the sky glowing with that orange which is the city's reflected light. It was like a furnace burning and turning, destroying everything which it touched, but becoming also a source of energy and light. He walked quickly back.

Laetitia woke up with a start: she had dreamt that someone was writing her name over and over again upon a steel wall. It was dark, and for a moment she thought she was in her hospital bed. She felt for Spenser in the space beside her. It was cold, empty. She looked at the clock: it was eleven. She called out to him, but he did not reply. She remembered that occasion when she had visited the flat in his absence – she had written him a note (what had it said?) and then torn it up.

The stillness and emptiness of this place seemed to her the same now – then, as a visitor, she had felt a stranger to it all. Now, too, she felt the same. She was excluded here – she had become a stranger in her own life. But, now that she understood that fact, she would live in accordance with it. She would make no plans for herself. She would drift with the great stream, as if her life were being carried for her by others.

She sat on the bed, and switched on the television. When Spenser returned from his long walk, he could hear the set blasting away – Letty, at least, he thought, is happy again.

twenty-seven

In the enforced lull in filming, while letters were issuing forth from Sir Frederick in his bureaucratic hat to the unions and from Sir Frederick in his film man's hat to Spenser, Spenser himself had telephoned Rowan Phillips and asked to see him. There were certain changes in the script which now seemed to him to be necessary, but these were really an excuse for the meeting. Spenser wanted his confidence in the film reinforced and Rowan was the only person who might provide such confirmation. For his part, Rowan was happy to discuss any changes Spenser might recommend: he would be gracious, cordial, ready to help, as long as he was paid extra for his trouble.

Spenser had decided that they should walk around the set which he had created by the river and which had now been left abandoned by the strike. Here were the warehouses and the alleys; Spenser had skilfully matched the old buildings with his own façades so that now the two were practically indistinguishable. Perhaps here it might be possible for Spenser to convince Rowan, and indeed himself, of the rightness of his conception.

And so they met, one afternoon in late spring, and walked beside the Thames together, towards the empty set of *Little Dorrit*. It was here that Spenser still planned to make the scene which would act as the final panoramic vision of the film – a view of London, crowded, packed with life, with the figures of Little Dorrit, Mr Dorrit and Little Mother the simpleton moving haphazardly through the crowd – but not lost within that crowd, rather sustained by its energy and momentum, feeling the impetus of a shared life.

Spenser Spender and Rowan Phillips walked among the empty warehouses, where their footsteps echoed and seemed to bounce across the river. They were like spectators walking through an empty gallery.

'And so you see the problem, Rowan,' Spenser was saying. 'If I give in to the unions, then I damage the film. If I don't give in, then I may lose it altogether. I'm caught in a trap. Caught in it.' He sighed and looked up at the walls of the warehouse which had been painted grey and black. Rowan Phillips entered Spenser's mood – it was the least he could do, under the circumstances.

'Well, it may not be a bad thing, Spenser. It gives us time for a re-think. I've been a little unhappy about parts of the script.'

'No, I think it was fine. Fine.' Spenser had forgotten that he was meant to ask Rowan for changes in it.

'It's nice of you to say so, Spenser, and I appreciate it. But there are passages that ring a little false. I tried to capture the spirit of Dickens, and I think I did at certain points, but some of it sounds hollow.'

'Well, you may be right.' (Rowan was annoyed at having his own sudden confession confirmed.) 'But don't worry about that, Rowan. The pictures will tell the real story.'

But, now that Rowan Phillips had begun the process of self-analysis, it would take a bandage applied across his mouth to stop him. It was such a rare event that he felt a responsibility to himself to carry it through – to lower the bucket to the bottom of the well, even if it should prove to be dry. In any case, he liked confessions of this sort. They relieved his conscience without touching it. 'I feel a bit of a fraud, Spenser, to tell you the absolute truth. I can't really see any proper way of bringing Dickens to life – he is not our contemporary, and it may have been a mistake to make him sound like one. Do you understand what I mean?'

In the brief heat of his self-analysis, he had forgotten that this was what Spenser had asked him to do.

Spenser merely nodded, and tried to smile. 'Go on, Rowan. I'm interested in this.' Like most people, he took Rowan at face value.

'Well, it might have been an illusion – an illusion on my part at least. To think that you could just take Dickens and bundle him into the twentieth century. We don't live in the same world. We don't even live in the same city—' He waved his hand across the river and, as if for the first time, Spenser noticed the tower blocks and the office complexes which rose above the familiar skyline. And then he looked at the set which he had created, half-real, half-artificial, its dark paint looming above him, and he felt a sudden disgust for it. A contempt for its hollowness and smallness. His original vision had turned into papier-mâché. He could not speak for a moment. 'And so you think, Rowan, the whole thing is a mistake. A mistake of some kind.' He sounded angry, but he was angry at himself.

'No, I didn't say that. I certainly didn't say that.' Rowan was alarmed: once again, his words had betrayed his feelings. 'I am only talking about my own contribution, Spenser, you know that's all I'm doing.' It was more of a plea than a statement.

'Still, Rowan, perhaps you're right. Perhaps the whole thing is just an expensive mistake. I never understood Dickens—'

And then they both heard confused noises – of shouting and running – somewhere close to them. They heard a voice screaming out, 'Here it is, boys! This is it! It can't be allowed, honest it can't!' The voice sounded manic – it was the kind of voice which made them stop and listen intently. It was Audrey's voice.

That morning, she had had an idea. She had been sitting, smoking a cigarette, hunched up in a chair with the shawl wrapped round her, staring at the burn in her carpet. It had been a lovely carpet, a deep shag, and now you couldn't help noticing that spot. It was their fault, getting her so worked up. No jobs, no prospects. How can I hide that spot? I can't let that whore pretend to be Little Dorrit. It isn't right, it isn't natural. All those lights and cameras. It's a mockery. She was half-heartedly stabbing at two flies with her lighted cigarette – the smoke, she thought, would clear them out – when the plan occurred to her. Tim was coming round to see her shortly, and she could hardly contain herself; she didn't know what she needed most, an audience or an accomplice. When he came through the door, sidling in and trying to guess her mood before he entered, she turned her back on him so that he could not see her expression of excitement. She tried to keep her voice level and conversational:

'You'll never guess, Tim, but I know how to get me own back. I just had this idea.'

'What idea is this, Aud?'

'I'm going to hit them where it hurts. That's what.'

'Hit them, Aud?'

Sometimes Tim got the uneasy feeling that he might be so drawn into her wild talk that one day he would start to believe it.

'Is that all you do, ask questions?'

'What do you mean, Aud – hit them?'

'I'm going to burn it down. Burn the whole lot down before they do any more damage – that lot, by the river.'

'I don't know what you're on about, Audrey.'

She was opening the window to let out the flies who, maddened by the smoke, were banging against the pane. Now she turned her face towards Tim, and it was exultant. 'I'm going to burn down that film place, that's what I'm going to do. Good riddance to bad rubbish, that's what it is.'

'But you can't do that, Audrey. You'll go to prison.'

'And what do you think I'm in already?'

'It's mad, Aud, it really is.'

'Oh mad, is it, Mr Cleverdick? I suppose you think I'm mad too, do you – mad Audrey? Madness, is it? Well, I'll show you.' She glared at him, and rushed out of the flat, picking up her handbag in the hall. As she did so, she turned around to Tim again. 'You don't have to stand on ceremony, Timothy Coleman, you can go home if you want to, you know. I won't be needing you.' Tim went to the door, and called out after her as she walked quickly down the steps towards the street.

He went back into the flat and sat down upon the sofa. He closed the window: it seemed chilly for spring, and a wind was coming up. He would wait here until she got back. It was just one of her notions. She'd be back in a minute, laughing at it all, saying she'd forgotten her fags in the excitement. He switched on the television.

Audrey walked out into the Borough High Street, her

160

handbag swinging open. She knew, from her first visit, exactly where the film set had been constructed and she knew that, on a Sunday, there would be no one to disturb her in her work. She was rummaging in her bag for a box of matches and, when she looked up, she saw some yards in front of her the group of tramps who generally loitered around the tube station. She had grown used to them now; she even liked them: their plight seemed very similar to her own. Now, for the first time, she went up to them. 'Excuse me, but can I have a word with you?'

They looked round at her, astonished. The young man with red hair put his hands in his pockets and cocked his head to one side as if to see her more clearly. 'Of course you can, missus. What can we do for you then?'

Audrey beckoned him over, and he walked slowly, casually, towards her. They were an incongruous sight – both of them red-haired, shabbily dressed, like characters in a Pierrot extravaganza. After a few minutes, the red-haired man sauntered back to the others.

'Do we all want to have a bit of fun then? A bit of a laugh? There's an old dump up the road she says she wants to burn down. She says it's okay.' They looked at her with a certain interest.

'What's it got to do with us?' one of them asked, looking at Audrey all the time although directing his question at the red-haired man.

'She says it's an old wooden stage which the rats have got to. She says it's a public nuisance. I say we can give her a hand.'

Since he had suggested it, they saw no reason to hang back. They had been neglected so universally and for so long that they no longer felt responsible for their actions. Whatever they did was of no consequence; what small bitterness or resentment they felt about their social destiny was generally directed against one another now, when they were drunk or cold. And so six or seven of them, led by the red-haired man, followed Audrey as she led the way towards Spenser Spender's film set. They took with them some rags, some old newspapers, two half-full bottles of methylated spirits. Audrey sang as she strode out in front, 'We're off to see the

Wizard, the wonderful Wizard of Oz!' But they walked
silently behind her. The few householders who saw them
stared for a moment and then, not wanting to attract the
tramps' attention, returned to their Sunday rituals.

As soon as they saw the chosen place, they knew there was
no harm in destroying it. It had been abandoned. It didn't
look right; it was false, flimsy. And, in addition, it was
making a mess of the area where they slept during the winter:
the old warehouses had been daubed with paint and chalked
letters. It was an eyesore, the red-headed tramp said, a
genuine eye-sore. They would be doing London a favour.
Audrey walked up to the painted wall of one of the
warehouses; she looked it up and down with a marked air of
satisfaction. 'Here it is boys!' she turned round to them where
they stood in a rather awkward and self-conscious group.
'This is it!' They still didn't move. 'It can't be allowed,
honest, it can't!'

Now, in a sudden rush of energy, they brought over their
rags and papers and piled them against the warehouse. The
red-headed tramp carefully carried the two bottles of spirit,
like a waiter. Audrey took out the box of matches from her
handbag and lit them one by one, throwing them, with an
almost disdainful gesture, upon the pile of spirit-soaked
material. It burnt slowly at first and then it erupted, the
flames sidling up against the paint and the wood of the
warehouse so that it became darker still, and blackened. A
cheer went up from the little group, as the wall bent and
crumpled into flame.

It was this cheer which sent Spenser Spender and Rowan
Phillips running towards the scene of the fire – a gust of wind
brought the noise to them as it brought them, also, the smell
of the smoke. They turned the corner of the alley and came
out by the river bank, to see one of the warehouses aflame and
in danger of setting light to the others. The smoke was
drifting through the alleys and passageways along the river.

Spenser Spender ran towards the strange group of tramps,
who now stood a little way back from the flames. 'Help me
put it out!' he shouted at them. The tramps had expected the
area to be deserted, and retreated in disorder as the running
man came closer to them. Spenser knew there was a

telephone box a few hundred yards away, within a small courtyard, and he ran through them. One of the tramps tripped him up. But in his panic he hardly seemed to know what was happening: he got to his feet, looked around bewildered, and hastened on to the telephone.

Audrey remained apart, looking at the fire, but now she scurried down one of the alleys between the warehouses, laughing. As she did so, she knocked against Rowan Phillips. They stared at each other, too startled by recognition to speak. Audrey ran on, and the smoke obscured her.

Spenser reached the telephone booth but, in his haste, could not find the door. And then, when he did so and grabbed the black receiver, the 'phone emitted a steady, low whistle – as if someone were blowing down the other end of the line, perhaps trying to fan the flames.

He left the telephone booth and ran back to the fire. It had spread over the entire warehouse. Rowan Phillips had backed away towards the river which, now at low tide, offered some kind of haven if the fire should spread too quickly. Spenser, seeing how it was drawing closer to the heart of his film set, grew frantic. If all this were destroyed, it would mean the end of *Little Dorrit*. 'For God's sake, Rowan!' he shouted into the wind which spun about the buildings. 'Help me control this thing!'

'Spenser, there's nothing we can do! It's taken a hold! Look at it – it's too enormous!'

Spenser rushed around to the side of the building, staring up at the flames as they drew nearer to his work, the project of his life. They were close to the huge canvas awning which had been the night sky. He ran towards it, coughing now with the smoke, and looking wildly around for Rowan. 'Rowan! Help me get this thing down before it gets caught in all this! Come on and help me!' But Rowan looked on silently, too frightened by the flames to move towards Spenser who was trying to disentangle the ropes and cables which kept the awning aloft. But the fire had reached it, and billowed across it; large lumps of molten tar and canvas began falling around Spenser and, before he could move away, the burning awning fell down on top of him. He made no cry or, if he did make one, it was muffled by the terrible sound of his set as it cracked and toppled – a sound like a huge wind, haunted, low. Rowan stood uncertain. If he moved quickly, he might be able to pull Spenser from beneath the awning. But he was afraid for his life, staring at the burning heap some thirty feet away from him. And then he saw Audrey standing to one side, just away from the centre of the fire. She must have seen what had happened to Spenser, but now she was staring at Rowan. He looked back at her. The heat seemed to be burning Rowan's skin. He put a hand up to his face and, with a conscious effort, he dragged himself away from Audrey's gaze. He ran beside the river, towards the road and pavement, away from the fire. As he ran, he heard Audrey laughing.

Tim heard the sound of the sirens above the murmur of the television, and he jumped up as though startled out of a profound sleep. He ran into the street without thinking, but he knew what had happened, and knew where he must go. The streets were filling up with people who could see the smoke rising in the distance, and Tim ran through them towards the Thames.

By the time he reached it, the fire had spread along the side of the river, warehouse after warehouse going up in the general conflagration. It was then that he saw Rowan, walking quickly away from the hoses and fire engines, looking straight ahead. He saw Tim, but his eye passed coldly over him. Tim understood, from that gaze, that something terrible had happened and he raced towards the fire. Large barriers had been erected, in the same area where Spenser had once erected his own, but Tim ducked underneath them, wrestled himself free from a fireman who attempted to stop him, and ran towards the burning buildings, calling out for Audrey. He knew that she would stay by her creation.

And she was there – in a small alley between two of the burning buildings. She was swaying to and fro, as large pieces of burning timber fell around her. She was trying to sing, but the smoke made her choke and retch. To get to her would mean going through the fire, or at least that spot it was likely to reach in a matter of seconds, but he did not hesitate. It was as if Tim saw his own life there, swaying between the flames, and he ran towards her. He dodged the flames, and smelt his clothes singe as he did so. Something hit his arm, but he felt no pain. He was close to Audrey now. 'Come towards me, Aud. Do you see me? Just come towards me.' But she did not seem to hear him; her eyes were closed, and she swayed from side to side. In one concentrated movement he ran towards her and gathered her up in his arms. She tried to fight him off, but in his panic and frenzy he held on too tightly for her to move. He ran out of the alley, through the haphazard flames, and towards the barrier. He felt her body relax in his arms when they reached the cooler air, as if she had drawn strength from the inferno, and when they reached the pavement he laid her gently on the ground. She was breathing peacefully now. Two ambulance men knelt over her and felt her pulse; they placed an oxygen mask over her face, and carried her away.

Tim turned towards the river, as if for relief. But it had become brilliant and fiery, taking on the shape and quickness of the flame. The city's skyline was hidden by smoke, and the surrounding neighbourhood was fully ablaze. A strong wind was blowing, pushing the flames forward. They burnt for a day and a night. It seemed to Tim then that they might burn for ever, taking the whole of London with them.

Spenser Spender lay dead in the ruins of *Little Dorrit*: he was the first victim of what came to be known as the Great Fire. The cause of the fire was never discovered, but it inflicted disaster and destruction upon the city, razing offices and homes, blasting the lives of those who worked and lived in them. It destroyed much that was false and ugly, and much that was splendid or beautiful. Some longed for it to burn everything, but for others a new and disquieting sense of impermanence entered their lives. Eventually, legends were to grow around it. It was popularly believed to have been a visitation, a prophecy of yet more terrible things to come.

twenty-eight

The news that there had been a strike by the film-crew was met by the prisoners with approval and amusement – any attempt to disrupt or dislodge the established world exhilarated them. When it was confirmed that they had left their equipment standing in the abandoned wing, Little Arthur danced upon his prison bunk. He knew about light and power. He would know what to do: if they were keeping his little sweet locked up, with her pale face and her grey dress just like a photograph, then he would rescue her. If she was not there, if they had carried her away in order to taunt him, then he would send the place crashing down.

'They won't know what hit them, Pally. The lowly will be exalted, won't they?' He had taken Pally's arm during an exercise period in the yard, and was skipping beside him like a child. 'It will be a fine thing, won't it, Pally, a fine thing!'

Pally wiped his mouth with his sleeve, which was a sign that he was about to say something. It was rare that he did so, and Little Arthur went up on tip-toe to hear him. 'Be c-c-careful of them, Arthur.' He looked seriously at the small man still dangling on his arm. 'They mean t-t-trouble.' He banged his chest with his fist, as if he were pointing to himself as living proof of what they could do.

'Oh don't mind that, my Pally-pal Pally. Wait and see. Wait and see.' They would all see, thought Little Arthur, and no two ways about it. He had made his plans, clocking them up in his head, banging his knees together as he imagined each move he would make, smiling at the easiness of it. He had brought Pally into it, just to share the excitement. They would do it next Sunday, during the free afternoon. The old wing, where they were keeping her among the lights and the fire, overlooked the prison exercise yard. He was so small, and

166

his limbs were so nimble, he would be over the wire fence in a jiffy.

And so, on that Sunday afternoon, the Sunday on which Audrey set fire to Spenser Spender's creation, the inmates of Little Arthur's landing were walking within the exercise enclosure. Some were sitting, smoking and looking up at the sky; others walked alone, their eyes always upon the ground. And then Pally, on cue, let out a terrible shriek and fell writhing on to the gravel path, kicking the dust up with his heels. The two officers superintending the prisoners ran over to him; one of them put his finger into his mouth which, in feigned mania, Pally bit harshly. The other prisoners had formed a semi-circle around Pally and were shouting advice.

In the confusion, Little Arthur walks slowly over to the metal fence and then climbs determinedly over it, his large hands gripping the wires. It only takes a short time. Once on the other side, and in the main prison yard, he hurries with his curious rolling gait towards the abandoned wing. He tests the door of the wing: it is still unlocked. Why lock an empty prison? The barred doors beyond the first entrance, rusty now with disuse, swing open as Little Arthur pushes them. He walks into the wing. He almost trips over one of the cables which have been left strewn across the floor and landings. A blue generator has been abandoned; the arc-light which had fallen still lies upon the ground. The equipment glints in the afternoon sunlight which filters in thin bars through the high windows of the wing, illuminating a bulb here, a painted backdrop there.

For Little Arthur, it is like returning to Fun City itself, a delight, a treasure-trove. But he is here to find his lost one; he clambers over the equipment and sings out, are you here, my dove? Where are you? His high voice disturbs the birds nesting in the roof, who fly out to look at him.

She has been taken away. They have left these electric relics to taunt him, to remind him of his old life among the lights and the power, a life now smashed and in ruins. He thinks he can hear voices in the distance – a whistle, perhaps, or a call – as though he were being pursued. He knows what to do: in the old days, when they came to look at him and

167

mock, he would hide in the electricity, hide in its glare. He climbs over some sound equipment, and finds two ends of cable unattached. He screws them together within their bright blue plastic mounting, and then hurries to the generator. There is the red handle, the same colour and size as his old switch in Fun City. Red for go, he used to say in the old days, red for go! He pulls down the switch, leaning upon it with his body to make the connection. As he does so, the current surges through the cables which Spenser Spender has left behind, and then, with a flash and a noise like tearing paper, the current is short-circuited by the fallen arc-light. The crackling and the sparkling are tremendous; it is as if Little Arthur has detonated an explosion. He stands amid the noise and the smoke, looking like a stage demon raised above the pit; he puts his hands over his ears, and grins.

The temporary generator within the wing has been connected with the main electric generator which is housed beneath the prison. The force of the shock which the short-circuit has provoked travels backward, bright and fiery like some avenging angel, and causes a failure within the electricity supply of the prison itself. The artificial illumination of the landings and the recreation areas, the hidden lighting within the punishment cells, the emergency signals within the prison hospital, the electronic locks which insulate each cell and each landing – all at once are broken.

As the lights go out, there is a huge roar from the prisoners, a spontaneous upwelling of feeling, like the sound of a train emerging at last from a tunnel. The cells are now open; the cameras, which had surveilled them, are shut down; the main gates and walls of the prison itself can be opened or scaled. Little Arthur, dancing in the old wing amongst the smoking equipment, has destroyed the current which had watched and imprisoned them.

Whilst some of the inmates sit disconsolate in their cells waiting for their lives to be set again upon an even court , while others whimper and turn their faces away from the freedom which beckons to them, the more ruthless or spirited of the inmates rush from their cell blocks and make for the main gate. Nothing can stop them: what had been barred has now been released, where there had been power there is now vacancy. There are few warders on duty on this Sunday afternoon, and they cannot halt them. No force on earth could have halted them, perhaps, in that moment when the system failed.

They stream out, the hesitant following the reckless in their movement towards freedom. Pally lurches among them, knocked this way and that, puzzled, frightened; but he knows that he must go, too. He runs back along the street where, a year before, he had passed Spenser Spender. Spenser, then, had been in the grip of his idea. Now, Little Arthur sits amongst the cables and laughs.

This is not a true story, but certain things follow from other things. And so it was that, on that Sunday afternoon, that same Sunday when Spenser Spender had died in the Great Fire caused by Audrey, Little Arthur set the prisoners free.

Peter Ackroyd was born in London in 1949. He was educated at Cambridge and Yale Universities, and worked as literary editor and managing editor of the *Spectator* from 1970 to 1981. He is the author of a number of collections of poetry, including *Country Life* and *London Lickpenny;* of many works of criticism and biography, including *Ezra Pound and His World* and *T.S. Eliot: A Life;* and of the novels *Hawksmore, The Last Testament of Oscar Wilde,* and *Chatterton.*